AN ADRIAN WEST THRILLER

THE
VENETIAN
KEY

L.D. GOFFIGAN

Copyright © 2022 by L.D. Goffigan

All rights reserved.

This book or any portion thereof may not be reproduced, or stored in a retrieval system, or transmitted in any form or by any means, electronic, mechanical, photocopying, recording, or otherwise, without the express written permission of the publisher.

ldgoffiganbooks.com

This is a work of fiction. Names, characters, organizations, places, events, and incidents are either products of the author's imagination or used fictitiously.

Printed in the United States of America

Paperback ISBN: 979-8-9902344-3-7

Cover Design by Mibl Art

PROLOGUE

Venice, Italy
May 1348

Jacomo Chiaveno struggled to walk through the streets of Venice, forcing his body to move step by step. He let out a cough, and bile ejected from his mouth, black and slimy, spilling onto the street below. He'd seen such phlegm from countless patients and known with absolute certainty that their time was limited to days. Sometimes hours.

And now it was his turn.

If he could have laughed, he would have, but the pain was too much. It was a miracle he could even walk. Around him, the streets were mostly abandoned. Those who dared to roam moved furtively, their heads lowered, faces pale with fear, as if the very act of walking through Venice's streets would cause the Death to strike them down as well.

It was hard to believe that only weeks before the Death had claimed Venice, it teemed with life, from its piazzas, churches, markets and streets, even its robust canals. As a member of one of the patrician families, he had enjoyed his life here, from the masked balls in which all were welcome as long as they wore masks, the delectable courtesans he'd partaken in, the exclusive dinners and meetings he'd participated in with other high-ranking men. Even his position as a physician was an agreeable one, using his medical knowledge to ease the suffering of his fellow Venetians, to prolong life as needed, or to ease into death when it was time. But death had held no dominance here in Venice, a city that teemed with life from all corners . . . not until recently. Now, no one was immune to its fatal call.

The ill, stricken with the Death, had once been confined to the islands of Poveglia, the Sacca Sessola, and Isola della Grazia, known to the Venetians as the *isoles del dolore*, the islands of sorrow. But once the numbers of the ill increased, all those afflicted were now here in Venice, their presence settling over the streets, a black curse, consuming the city like a ravenous beast.

It was all because of him. *This was supposed to be for the enemies of Venice. Not the women, the children, the innocent.* Yet deep down in the depths of his soul, he knew that even his enemies had not deserved such a death. No one did.

Now this cursed blight would destroy them all.

There were some who thought the Death was divine punishment for Venice's vices; its love of money and peddling of flesh, the ruthless increase of its empire at the cost of the lands—and lives—that surrounded it. They believed the Death was the price for all of Venice's resplendent glory.

Jacomo knew exactly what had caused all of this suffering.

Pain shot through him and he nearly stumbled to his knees, but he forced himself forward. From a nearby window, he could hear mournful weeping; he didn't know if it was from the dying, or from one of those left behind. He kept moving, the wailing a fitting background for his final journey. Soon, his spirit would drift off to its rightful place in hell.

But first, one last task. One last attempt to right this horrendous wrong, to stop this blight, to save them all.

It seemed as if he'd been walking forever when he found what he was looking for. He approached, a multitude of emotions coursing through him.

The key, he thought, resolution filling him. *This must all end. It must be destroyed.*

Jacomo closed his eyes before stepping inside, knowing that this was the place where he would draw his last breath.

CHAPTER 1

Present Day
Venice, Italy
6:47 PM

*A*drian West looked out at the rippling waters of the Grand Canal. The sun was dipping low into the horizon, setting the sky ablaze in a stunning array of colors ranging from lavender to deep orange. The cool evening breeze that drifted from the canal caressed her skin as her partner, Nick Harper, moved in close behind her, wrapping his arms around her waist. Adrian closed her eyes, allowing herself to pretend—for just a moment—that she and Nick were on a romantic vacation, enjoying Venice and each other.

She opened her eyes, expelling a sigh. If only that were true.

Two weeks ago, on the heels of a case that had led to the revelatory find of a historical Atlantis, she'd received a note with a mysterious anagram pointing her to Venice.

The key you seek lies in the floating city.

She'd debated going to FBI headquarters to run forensics on the letter, but something told her to keep it to herself. Instead, she and Nick had informed their boss, Jeremy Briggs, at the newly formed Relics and Antiquities Task Force, that they were taking a much needed vacation after their latest case.

Since arriving in Venice, she and Nick had been on a feckless scavenger hut, trying to find what the mysterious sender had wanted her to discover. The first couple of days they'd waited at their hotel, hoping that the sender would simply approach them. When that hadn't happened, she'd analyzed the letter over and over again, searching for any other clue as to what she should look for. They'd resorted to seeking out place names in the city that could relate to keys or locks, visiting the famous old prisons beneath the Doge's Palace, the ruler of the old Venetian Republic, in the Piazza San Marco, and interrogating museum docents about any symbolic place in Venice that could relate to keys or locks. But so far they'd come up empty.

After nearly two weeks of fruitless searching, she wondered if this was all an elaborate prank.

Perhaps someone out there toying with her after her recent public successes. She hadn't told Nick, but a part of her was considering giving up the search. They couldn't stay in Venice forever; the task force would need them back soon.

"I can hear your thoughts, West," Nick said gently, turning her to face him. "What's going on?"

Adrian smiled. Her partner knew her too well. She reached up to press a gentle kiss to his lips, glad that she could now openly express her feelings for him. She and Nick had always shared a deep friendship that bordered on the romantic when they were partners during her initial stint with the bureau. When they'd reconnected after Adrian returned to law enforcement, it was as if that friendship had been set aflame. A burning attraction hummed between them like a current, an attraction they hadn't acted on until their most recent case. Their romantic relationship was still new, and Adrian was relieved at how easily they'd made the transition from friends to lovers.

"I'm thinking that this all feels like a dead end. Do you think we should head back to DC?" she asked.

"I'll leave that up to you," Nick replied after a brief pause. "But I think someone left you that note for a reason."

Adrian nodded, though frustration filled her. He was right . . . she just didn't know where else to look.

Nick tugged on her hand, leading her away from their spot overlooking the Grand Canal and back through the bustling Saint Mark's Square, where a crowd had gathered to take in the sunset, toward their hotel.

Venice had many nicknames due to its unique beauty and its gloried history as a major player on the world stage, from La Serenissima, the most serene, to Queen of the Adriatic. There was also the Floating City, an homage to the multiple islands that made up the city, and City of Masks, for the array of masks that appeared during the city's annual celebration of carnival.

Adrian's personal nickname for Venice was the Timeless City, because there was something that was timeless about it. Every time she visited Venice, she felt as if she was transported back through time. Most streets and buildings had remained the same after centuries, and the absence of cars truly made her feel as if she was in the past. There was something almost otherworldly about the myriad of canals that wound its way through the city like a spider's intricate web, connecting the *sestieres*—districts—and various historic squares.

Their hotel was in the southernmost part of the Cannaregio sestiere, one of the larger districts that teemed with tourists and locals alike. It was dotted with a multitude of sights that included *palazzos* from the city's Golden Age and a myriad of medieval churches. As they drew close to their hotel, a former palazzo that had belonged to a wealthy Venetian family, Adrian slowed her pace, noticing a man hovering in front of it. He was oddly focused on the third floor, the same floor she and Nick were staying on.

Though they were still some distance away, and she could only make out a tall frame and dark hair . . . there was something familiar about him. Something that she couldn't place, but the sensation made the hairs on the back of her neck stand up. Without thinking, Adrian removed her hand from Nick's and quickened her pace, approaching the man.

But the man quickly turned and walked away, disappearing into a throng of approaching tourists. Instinct made Adrian turn her pace into a jog, ignoring the annoyed looks of the tourists as she maneuvered around them to trail the man. Up ahead, she saw him veer out of the crowd and abruptly turn into a *callette*—a small Venetian alleyway.

The crowd of tourists seemed to thicken, and she had to make her way around them until the crowd thinned. Only then could she turn into the callette.

Despite the bustle of tourists that filled most of the streets of Venice, this callette was empty, the back doors of the buildings that lined it shut, the windows closed . . . though she swore she felt eyes on her. Nick joined her as she ventured further down the callette, but there was no sign of the mysterious man—or anyone else. It simply came to a dead end.

Another wave of frustration coursed through her. It was probably just a tourist, or even a local. Taking one last look around, she and Nick headed out of the callette.

"I thought I saw someone," Adrian said, answering his silent question. Embarrassment washed over her. Was she so desperate that she was now following random people in the hope of some connection?

"I saw him too," Nick reassured her, reaching out to squeeze her hand. "You've not gone totally crazy."

"Just a little," Adrian returned, grinning.

"OK. A tad."

As she and Nick were about to enter their hotel, a young man who couldn't be older than nineteen bumped into her. He muttered an apology in Italian before disappearing around the next corner.

It was only when they were in the safety of their room that Adrian reached into her pocket, taking out the flyer that the kid had subtly slipped there. She had instantly felt him put something in her pocket, but kept her expression neutral in case they were being followed.

"Way to be subtle," Nick said with an annoyed snort, as Adrian unfolded the flyer—a pizza flyer.

"This isn't just a flyer," Adrian murmured, holding it up.

At the very bottom, scrawled out in dark black ink, was a series of letters.

OAADCASURGMRTONNDODAAN-
DUSTORATT
ENCTNANDABDSAPPAOSREDORNT

CHAPTER 2

International Conference for Synthetic Biology
(ICSB)
Geneva, Switzerland
8:15 PM

"As we move into the future, the field of synthetic biology will expand. We can utilize the modernity of technology along with the very basics of ancient, biological life to work in tandem as opposed to against each other. And as artificial intelligence tools intensify, the field will only grow stronger, benefiting us all. And that is why this field—our field—is the future."

Doctor Vittoria Trivisana took a step back from the podium as she concluded her speech, keeping the smile pinned on her face as the hundreds of attendees gathered in the auditorium gave her thunderous applause. She turned to leave the stage, offering a polite smile to the next speaker who moved toward the podium, though it faded when her bodyguard, Isabella, approached.

Not many scientists had bodyguards, but her family's wealth had made her a target since she was a child. When she was younger, she had fantasized about being able to move about without the watchful eye of her family's personal security service. That had been her intention, when she'd initially gone into the field of synthetic biology, living her life on her own terms as a scientist without the pressure of the Trivisana family name.

That had all changed several years ago. Everything had changed several years ago. Now she needed bodyguards, and for more than her wealth. Ever since she'd made that fateful decision to take up her family's hidden cause, bodyguards were a necessity. Isabella was a trustworthy associate who knew everything about her and the organization that they were both a part of. With Isabella's nearly six-foot frame and lean, muscular build, she was an intimidating figure to both men and women.

Isabella's expression was grim, and Vittoria's heart filled with dread.

"What is it?" Vittoria asked, tense.

Isabella took her by the arm, leading her away from the small crowd gathered backstage.

"It's Adrian West," she said, her voice low, once they were away from the others. "She's been spotted in Venice. Our associate believes she's been there for some time."

Vittoria stiffened. She and her other colleagues were very aware of Adrian West. West's most recent case had put her on their radar.

A chill spread down her spine. Did West somehow know of their plans? How could she, if so? Had there been a leak?

"Thank you," Vittoria said, forcing a calm into her voice that she didn't feel. "Stay on her. I'll inform the others."

Vittoria wanted to head to Venice immediately, but she had to keep up appearances. There was a drinks event to attend after the speeches and colleagues to mingle with.

She moved away from Isabella, though she could feel her bodyguard's watchful eye on her as she dutifully mingled, forcing herself to converse and laugh with her colleagues. It was important that she keep up appearances, to hide her true cause.

But the whole time her mind was on her and her associates' plans . . . and on Adrian West's mysterious presence in Venice.

When Vittoria could finally leave, Isabella trailing, she took out her phone, sending an encrypted message to the others.

> Adrian West is in Venice.

> We need to discuss.

Venice, Italy
8:22 PM

ADRIAN STUDIED the series of letters at the bottom of the flyer. It was likely another anagram.

"Is it so hard for this person to just tell us what they mean without codes or anagrams?" Nick muttered, letting out a frustrated curse.

Adrian offered him a smile, placing the flyer down on the desk. "Well, hopefully this is an easy one to crack."

Adrian and Nick buckled down and worked for a couple of hours, using different letter and word combinations, even using online anagram scramblers, but nothing comprehensible came up.

"My brain is fried, and I'm going to guess yours is too," Nick said at around midnight, rubbing his eyes. "We need to rest."

"I'm going to keep going," Adrian muttered, jotting down yet another word combination. She could feel Nick's eyes on her; he knew when she got into obsessive mode, it had happened many a time during their casework as partners during their early days at the bureau, and he'd learned the hard way to pick his battles.

Adrian kept working until another hour had passed, and she could hear Nick's soft snoring. Frustrated, she leaned back in her chair, rubbing her eyes. Fatigue was settling over her, affecting her ability to think.

Adrian stood, moving over to the window, looking down at the cobblestoned streets below, which were now mostly empty except for the stray tourist stumbling back to the hotel. She needed to sleep to help her focus, but her mind still whirred. Who was this mysterious sender? Had it been that man from earlier after all? What did he want with her? What did these messages mean?

Adrian shook her head as if to clear it. Nick was right. She would sleep and then get back to it in the morning.

She made her way to the bathroom after changing into her pajamas, and as she squeezed toothpaste onto her toothbrush, she froze.

Closing her eyes, she let out a curse. How could she not have thought of this before?

She scrambled out of the bathroom, making her way to the notepad she'd left on the desk. She tore off a new sheet of paper, working out several more word patterns. As she did, a clear pattern emerged.

Adrian kept working, adrenaline fueling her now, until she finally worked out the message.

"OK," Nick said, causing her to jump. She looked up. She'd been so focused on her work that she hadn't noticed the sky starting to light up outside. He was sitting up in bed, rubbing sleep out of his eyes as he gave her a scolding look.

"Adrian—"

"I figured out the message," she interrupted. "I

should have seen it before. It would have saved us loads of time. The message isn't in English—it's in Italian. The sheer number of vowels, something much more common in Italian than English," she said, irritated with herself. Of the languages she spoke, Italian was the most vowel rich, the closest of the Romance languages to its Latin origins. "*Ci incontriamo a Ragusa presso il santo patrono. Attenti stanno guardano.*"

Nick spoke Italian as well, but Adrian's excitement propelled her to translate. "We meet in Ragusa at the patron saint. Careful, they're watching."

CHAPTER 3

"<i>R</i>agusa?" Nick echoed after a brief pause. "They're watching? Who are they?"

"Good question," Adrian said grimly, looking down at the message she'd decoded.

Ragusa sounded vaguely familiar, but she didn't know why. She took out her phone, plugging the word into an Internet search, and it immediately answered her question.

"Dubrovnik. In Croatia," she said. "Ragusa was its name for quite some time."

"So now the mystery sender wants us to go to Dubrovnik?" Nick asked warily, heaving a sigh.

Adrian looked down at the note, understanding his wariness. The first anagram she'd received had sent them here, and they'd not found a hint of who sent them here or why. Now this same person—and she was assuming it was the same person—wanted them to go to Croatia? Doubt tingled along her spine, and she again wondered if this was some elaborate prank. Why hadn't the sender just shown themselves by now? Why go to the trouble of sending them another message to go to yet another location?

A thought suddenly struck her. "That man we saw yesterday," Adrian said, recalling the mysterious man they'd pursued outside their hotel. "He may have been the sender after all."

"Maybe he saw that someone was watching us?" Nick suggested. "I still wish he'd just approach us directly and tell us what the hell is going on."

"I know. But like you said, there has to be a reason he's being so cautious." She glanced back down at her phone, where she'd pulled up a map of Croatia. "Dubrovnik is a quick flight from here. Nick . . . you don't have to come," she added quickly. "These messages are for me. You've already done more than enough. And if this is all for—"

"Hey," Nick interrupted, leveling her with a firm stare. "We're a team. Partners in more ways than one. You know that. Where you go, I go."

Adrian smiled, warmth filling her. She'd made the suggestion knowing he'd never leave her to handle this on her own, but his words moved her all the same.

"Are you going all romantic on me, Nick Harper?"

"Only for you, West," he returned, his lips turning up in a smile. He glanced back down at the flyer, his tone turning serious. "I just wonder—why Dubrovnik?"

"I don't know," Adrian said slowly. "I do know that Dubrovnik was once a colony of the Venetian Republic when it was a powerful city state, so there is a connection."

"The message also mentions meeting at a patron saint. What do you think that refers to?"

"It has to be some sort of landmark pointing us where to go. I'm assuming a patron saint of the city," she said.

They moved to Adrian's laptop and performed a quick online search, discovering that the patron saint of Dubrovnik was Saint Blaise, who in the tenth century had rescued the citizens of Dubrovnik from, ironically, invading Venetians.

"There's Saint Blaise's Church," Nick said, reading over her shoulder as she pulled up a list of landmarks related to the patron saint. "Looks like it's a major tourist attraction. Which means crowds. Which means—"

"Easier to blend in," Adrian murmured. "Easier to meet someone there and get lost in the crowds if we're being watched."

Adrian turned, meeting Nick's eyes. For the first time in weeks, they had a solid lead. Still, nervousness filled her. Her gut instinct told her that time was of the essence to find out what the sender had contacted her for, and they were running out of it.

CHAPTER 4

Vrânceanu Institute of Historical Archaeology
Bucharest, Romania
11:30 AM

Doctor Polina Lysenko hummed along to the pop song playing in her headphones as she examined genetic sequencing data extracted from a bone sample on her laptop. The lab around her was mostly empty. Most of her colleagues were out in the field and Polina was happy to have the lab to herself. Though necessary in her line of work, she wasn't enthusiastic about field work, preferring her time in the lab to analyze and study samples on her own.

As a paleopathologist, examining relics from the ancient past was her favorite thing to do, as odd as it seemed. Ever since she was a child, the past—and bones—had fascinated her, something that had initially caused her traditional Romanian parents concern. They had probably hoped it was just a childhood quirk, but Polina had made the study of old bones and pathogens her life's work, studying bioarchaeology at the University of Bucharest and earning her PhD in anthropology at Oxford.

She jotted down notes about the data on her tablet, clicking over to the next screen to examine the next sample. This had been arbitrary work so far, with all the samples containing the exact same genetic material, making her job easy. She tapped her feet to the music, studying the sample, prepared to jot down the same notes.

Except . . . this sample was different. It bore a slightly different genetic signature. She studied it for a long time, as if it would suddenly make sense on its own. But it wasn't changing. This sample was definitely different from all the others.

Frowning, she made a note of this, clicking through the samples until she found another one which bore the same, but different, signature. And another. Another. *Another*.

Polina took off her headphones, drumming her fingers on the desk. These samples were collected from bones found in a fourteenth century mass grave outside of Feodosia, on the Crimean Peninsula. Perhaps the extraction team had accidentally swapped some of the bone samples? She swiveled in her chair, turning to face the direction of her boss' office, which she could see through the glass windows of the lab. Mikhail's door was open, and he was on his laptop, his brow furrowed in concentration.

He seemed to feel her eyes on him and looked up, giving her a smile that was decidedly lecherous. Annoyed, Polina averted her gaze. Mikhail hadn't been shy about making his interest in her clear, and Polina had concertedly avoided being alone with him. But this was important, and she needed to discuss her findings with him.

Heaving a sigh, she stood and made her way over to his office. Mikhail leaned back in his chair, practically licking his lips. Polina forced herself not to roll her eyes.

"Doctor Lysenko," he purred. "How can I help you?"

"I've been studying the bone samples from the Feodosia field find, and there's something strange. Some of them are genetically different from the others. Is it possible the samples got mixed up somehow?"

His lecherous gaze immediately dissipated, and he straightened, studying her with urgency. "How are they different?"

"They seem to be completely different strains of the same pathogen, but that shouldn't be possible. The dating confirmed that the people buried at the site were all interred at the same time in the same place, so why would there be different strains?"

Mikhail was silent for several long moments,

not looking at her as he seemed to consider something.

"Yes, it sounds like there may have been a mistake. Perhaps some contamination. But just in case, I'll look them over with Doctor Ilieş for further examination."

Now it was Polina's turn to stiffen. She and Doctor Florin Ilieş were colleagues on the same level with the same amount of experience, though Florin acted as if he had decades of experience on her. "Are you sure? I can take—" she began.

"Yes," he said shortly. "Send your data over to Doctor Ilieş immediately. You can handle the samples that just came in from the university instead."

Polina frowned. She felt as if she were being punished for her discovery. Mikhail's expression was now hard, as if daring her to contradict him.

She gave him a stiff nod and left his office, though unease had slithered up her spine.

Something wasn't right.

~

Dubrovnik, Croatia
2:07 PM

DUBROVNIK, which lay on the southwestern coast of Croatia on the Adriatic Sea, was a city with an old and varied history. Founded in the seventh century by refugees from nearby Greek colonies, it eventually flourished under the Byzantine Empire before coming under the control of the Venetian Republic. Over the centuries, given its strategic position, it was ruled by other great powers of their respective times, from the French to the Hapsburg empires.

Adrian and Nick had arrived in Dubrovnik after a short flight from Venice, taking care to make certain they weren't being followed, checking into their hotel under assumed names. They were making their way from their hotel, located just north of Old Town, toward Saint Blaise's Church.

As they drew closer to the church, Adrian knew that her instinct about why the sender had sent them here was correct. Throngs of tourists filled the square surrounding the church; it was very easy to blend in here.

Her gaze shifted to the church, taking in its Baroque architecture. Built on the remains of an older, damaged medieval church in the eighteenth century, the church itself had a link to Venice. The architect, a Venetian artist by the name of Marino Gropelli, had modeled it after the church of San Maurizio in Venice, which Adrian and Nick had visited during their time in the city. She wondered if the sender had sent them here with this link in mind.

They found a tucked away corner on the southwest section of the church, pretending to peruse the guidebooks they'd picked up from the airport, trying their best to look like tourists. They did this for some time, subtly checking the crowds around them, but no one seemed to pay any particular attention to them. They even moved locations several times, gradually making their way around the entirety of the church and continuing to check their surroundings.

After two hours of this, Adrian was worried that they were in the wrong place. She thought about the message that had sent them here. *We meet in Ragusa at the patron saint. Careful, they're watching.* The message had been clear—the patron saint. But there were many statues of the patron saint in Dubrovnik.

"Are you thinking what I'm thinking?" Nick asked.

"Yeah. We're probably be in the wrong place," she replied with a heavy sigh. "We need to think about other locations."

"There's another place nearby that we can try," Nick said, handing her his guidebook and pointing at a passage. "Ploče Gate. That's where another statue of the patron saint is."

Adrian hesitated, looking around. What if they were in the right place and left just as the sender arrived? "Maybe I should go, and you—"

"No," Nick interrupted with a scowl. "I'm not trying to pull the protective boyfriend card, but we don't know anything about this person. What if it's a trap? It's best if both of us go."

"That *is* the protective boyfriend card," Adrian

returned, smiling, but held her hands up in acquiescence. "But I won't argue with you."

They took one last look around before leaving the church, making their way through the crowds of tourists to the entrance of Old Town, where Ploče Gate was located.

Built during the fourteenth century, Ploče Gate consisted of a bridge with a stone balustrade that led to Luza Square, one of the most popular squares of Dubrovnik. The statue of Saint Blaise was just above the entrance. Another protective fortress, Revelin Fortress, made up the Ploče Gate entrance, providing another layer of protection to both Dubrovnik and its harbor.

She and Nick found another corner, again pretending to consult their guidebooks as they watched the throngs of tourists and locals alike wander through and around the gates.

An hour passed, and Adrian's stomach grumbled in protest; she had barely eaten during their day of travel. Frustration began to rise, and she wondered again if this was all for naught. Had they come to the right place? Were they even in the right city? And what if this was in fact some elaborate practical joke? Her frustration was at its highest ebb when she spotted a man emerging from the shadows of the gate opposite them.

Adrian stilled as he drew closer. The blood drained from her face as he came within a recognizable distance. She could feel her heart pounding in her ears, and the world around her seemed to fade away.

The man who approached her was a dead man.

The dark hair she had once been so familiar with was now mostly gray. The once warm, brown eyes were now both shadowed and haunted.

The man was her father.

A torrent of emotions flooded her body as she swayed on her feet, and the ground rushed toward her.

CHAPTER 5

Alexandria, Virginia
4:15 PM

Cora West had the unnerving sensation that someone was following her.

That sense had lingered as she'd carried out her errands for the day, going to the grocery store and then the bank, a prickling of unease that trailed her. By the time she'd returned home, pulling her car into her driveway, her heart was hammering, and she scanned her rearview mirror for what seemed like the millionth time that day. But other than the occasional car passing by and a young woman walking her dog, there was no one.

Cora expelled a breath. *Snap out of it.* Her daughter, Adrian, would actually be proud of her alertness. Adrian's years in law enforcement had taught her that you could never be too careful. But

Adrian was also overly cautious because of what had happened to her father.

At the thought of Robert, a shard of grief splintered Cora's chest. She closed her eyes for a moment, expelling another breath before getting out of the car to grab her groceries. She was just on edge because of all the worrying she did for Adrian now that she was officially back with the FBI.

Her brave, adventurous daughter had only recently returned to the States before leaving again, this time to vacation in Venice with her partner turned boyfriend, Nick Harper. Cora's lips twitched in a smile as she thought of Adrian and Nick. Cora had always seen the connection that hummed between them. She was glad they had finally seen it, too. Besides, she adored Nick. She knew he loved Adrian and would take could care of her. Together, they would give her adorable grandchildren, something she'd hinted at more than once, which caused her daughter endless annoyance.

Cora chuckled to herself, trying to imagine Adrian as a suburban mom, a vision so ridiculous she had to shake her head. Feeling more relaxed now, she unlocked the front door and headed inside, dropping her shopping bags on the kitchen counter. Adrian was now on her mind, so she took out her phone and sent a quick text to her little girl —who hated it when she called her that.

> Hope you and Nick are enjoying Venice. I want photos ASAP.

Just as she was putting down her phone, she heard it.

A soft click. It came from the living room, where the patio door led out to the backyard.

Cora's heart leapt into her throat. She recalled what Adrian had once told her. *If you ever think there's an intruder in the house, get out first, call for help later.*

She was already racing out the kitchen toward the front door when a hard male body slammed into her from behind, clamping a firm hand over her mouth.

∼

Dubrovnik, Croatia
8:52 PM

ROBERT WEST HOVERED OVER ADRIAN, his eyes raking over her still form with worry.

After she'd collapsed at the sight of him, Nick Harper had rushed forward, taking her into his arms, demanding to know who the hell he was.

"I'm her father," he'd said simply. Nick had paled, but returned his focus to Adrian.

"We need to get her off the street," he'd muttered. "And then you have a hell of a lot of explaining to do."

They'd taken her back to their hotel in a cab, and now Nick was seated next to her as she lay down on the bed, clutching her hand in his.

"Was there anyway you could have told her you were still alive in a different, less cryptic way? You know, one that didn't have us running all over the world and then causing her to pass out?" Nick demanded, glaring at him.

Shame and guilt filled Robert. He had gone over how he would approach her a million times, but there didn't seem any right way to do it. No matter what, he knew that the best way would be in person . . . otherwise, she simply wouldn't believe it. And the notes were necessary. He didn't know how closely they were watching her.

She didn't know how much danger she was in.

He opened his mouth to speak, but Nick held up his hand, scowling. "Save the explanations for your daughter."

Robert nodded, his gaze returning to Adrian's face. Though he'd watched her from afar over the years, it was still surreal to see her up close, and his throat clogged with emotion. She had grown into a beautiful woman and was the spitting image of her mother, Cora. It had been nearly impossible to stay away from them both, to let them believe he was gone forever, but he'd done what was necessary to keep them safe—and alive.

Soon, Adrian stirred, and Nick smiled at her in relief.

"I didn't take you for the fainting damsel type, West," Nick said, squeezing her hand. Adrian groggily returned his smile, but it faltered when her gaze shifted to Robert. The memory of seeing him seemed to slam into her, and she paled.

She stared to stand, but Nick reached out to stop her. "Easy, soldier," he said gently. "You're still in shock."

Adrian's gaze remained on Robert, her face a storm of emotions—disbelief, anger, fear, relief. Her gaze raked over his features; she was taking in every detail of his face, the face she hadn't seen for over a decade, one he knew she never thought she'd see again.

She stumbled to her feet, ignoring Nick's restraining hand on her arm, her voice shaking.

"Explain." Her voice ended on a strangled sob, hinging on pain and rage. "Explain. *Right now.*"

CHAPTER 6

Ten Years Ago

It all began with the suicide of Niles Harrington.

Niles had been one of Robert's closest friends; he was like a brother to him. Like Robert, he was a professor who held a doctorate in ancient languages, which was his life's passion. They'd met during their undergraduate years at Harvard and stayed in touch long after graduating, even though they lived in different cities and taught at different universities—Niles at Harvard, Robert at Georgetown. Niles was a lifelong bachelor; he'd once told Robert that a partner would only get in the way of his academic pursuits. Because of Niles' preference for solitude, Robert was his closest friend and therefore his emergency contact.

And so, it was Robert whom the police notified

when Niles was found dead by suicide in his home in Cambridge.

As soon as the police told him the cause of death, Robert knew something was amiss. Niles had no history of depression or any mental illness, nor he was he in any financial straits. He didn't even need to work as a professor as he'd inherited money from his family; he worked purely for the joy of it.

At the time of Niles' death, he was at the peak of his professional career, having just gotten tenure and shortlisted for a Neil and Saras Smith Medal for his achievements in the linguistics field. Robert's wife, Cora, and other friends of his assured him that no one could ever truly see the signs, but Robert wasn't convinced. He firmly believed that his lively, passionate best friend hadn't taken his own life.

In the weeks after Niles' death, he'd done his own investigation, not telling anyone what he was up to; he didn't want to worry his wife or their daughter, Adrian, who was away at college.

The authorities had given him Niles' possessions, including his laptop. Robert had a tech savvy colleague of his at Georgetown uncover old online searches that Niles had tried to wipe clean.

Niles was looking into a secret society with origins that stretched back to the Greco-Roman period—one that still existed today. Niles' notes consisted of several high-profile murders . . . all suicides. A doctor in Venice, Italy. A historian in

Aswan, Egypt. A professor in Paris, France. Niles seemed convinced that this society had something to do with each of these suicides, which he believed were, in fact, murders. This chilled Robert to the bone. If Niles was right, the same people had gotten to him.

After combing through all of Niles' notes, he found the contact info of a man who was a purported ex-member of this organization, who only went by the name Caesar. By some miracle, the mystery man agreed to talk to Robert, as he'd been one of the last people Niles had spoken to before his death. But his conditions were firm. Robert had to come to him where he lived in Istanbul, and not tell anyone the true purpose of his visit.

Robert obliged, telling Cora and Adrian that he was going to Istanbul to research a book he was writing on the origins of Proto-Indo-European languages. He felt guilty for lying to them, but his gut told him it was best to keep them out of this; the people he was dealing with were dangerous. This was something that he needed to do to get to the bottom of what really happened to Niles. He owed it to the man he loved like a brother.

He barely slept on the direct flight from DC to Istanbul, nervous anticipation humming through his veins, praying that he would find answers. He was jittery by the time the plane landed at the Istanbul Atatürk Airport in the late afternoon, and as he left the arrivals terminal, paranoia arose in his gut. The hairs on the back of his neck stood up; he felt as if every passerby he walked by was staring at him. Gripping the handle of his bag, anxiety swirled in his belly. Robert told himself that he was just on edge. He just needed to talk to Caesar and get some answers.

He left the international arrivals area, making his way to the rendezvous point just outside the parking lot where Caesar was to pick him up. His breathing calmed as a dark blue sedan approached. *Finally*.

The car stopped, the back door and trunk opening automatically. Robert loaded his suitcase into the truck and entered the car.

Yet as soon as the door shut behind him, he knew something was terribly wrong.

An elegant, dark-haired woman in her fifties sat in the back seat, giving him a frosty smile. Despite her aura of refinement, there was something dangerous about the way she looked at him. Something that unnerved him.

"Doctor West," she said cooly, her words shaped with a rich Italian accent. "I know you have many questions. But we have many for you as well."

Robert licked his dry lips, his heart hammering with rising panic. He put his hand on the car door handle. "Who are you? Where is—"

Before he could complete his sentence, she reached toward him, jabbing something into the side of his neck, and his world faded to black.

CHAPTER 7

When Robert came to, the same woman stood in front of him. He was seated in a chair, his wrists and legs bound. He was in a spacious study, filled to the brim with overflowing bookshelves, the walls dotted with expensive-looking paintings. The curtains were drawn, so he couldn't see where he was, but he didn't hear the sounds of a bustling city outside. It was jarringly quiet. He had the feeling he was far from Istanbul.

"You are a lucky man," the woman said. She was giving him a polite smile, though there was an edge to it, like a dagger carving into flesh. "To have such a beautiful wife and daughter. Cora. Adrian. Such lovely women."

Terror flooded every part of him. Instinctively, he jerked against his bonds. The woman's smile disappeared, her expression turning hard.

"I will make this short, as there is much work

ahead of us. I know you've been looking into us, I know what you've found, and I also know you're foolishly planning on going to the authorities. My colleagues want you killed, just like your annoying friend Niles, but I believe they were too hasty. We could have used his expertise. I think you can also be useful to us—alive, if you make the right choice. I will make you a proposition, and you will give me an answer here and now."

She turned as an intimidating, broad-shouldered man entered the room, holding a pistol at his side. He calmly leveled it at Robert's head.

"You will work for us," the woman said. "You do this, or you will die now. Not only that, but your lovely wife and daughter will be tortured, quite thoroughly, before we kill them. You've been looking into us; you know what we are capable of. I need your answer, Doctor West."

In his mind's eye, he saw the image of his wife's face and his daughter . . . his little girl. His heart clenched. There was no choice here.

"Yes," he whispered.

The woman smiled, not looking surprised, but her expression was still cold, as she continued, "I know what you're thinking. As soon as our guard slips, you will reach out to your family, get the authorities involved, go into hiding. But know this. We are *everywhere*. There is no hiding from us. No escaping. You even think about going against us and I will know. I will start with your daughter, and she will be in pieces by the time I'm finished with her. I will make your wife watch. Your wife will be next. This is not a bluff, Doctor West. I assure you, it gives me no pleasure to make such threats. I just want to make certain that our partnership is fruitful. Do you understand?"

"I understand," Robert said shakily. "Can I—is it possible for me to say goodbye, to—"

"No," the woman interrupted. "As of this moment, you are dead to them. You are dead, so they may live."

You are dead, so they may live.

It was a statement that Robert repeated to himself over the next days, weeks, months . . . years. It echoed in his mind as he changed his appearance, shaving his head and putting in contacts, changing his name to the fake identity the organization, which he soon learned was called the Dieci, provided for him. He repeated it as he traveled to remote parts of the globe, using his expertise in rare and ancient languages to help the Dieci translate various old writings and decrypt codes and ciphers, ranging from encrypted letters to ancient temple markings.

He managed to catch fleeting glimpses of his wife and daughter with the help of Oliver, a tech whiz and a friend he made through the Dieci, gazing at their images during many lonely days and nights, continuing to repeat the mantra to himself. *You are dead, so they may live.* Oliver would also periodically give him updates about them, telling him about Adrian joining the FBI, which he knew, deep down, was about him. He worried for her, and was relieved when she left the bureau to work in academia, following in his footsteps by teaching linguistics.

Oliver was a young Englishman in his late twenties and referred to himself as a professional hacker; he'd gotten involved in illegal circles that involved financial fraud and black market money transactions. The Dieci found him through his black market activities, forcing him to use his skills for the organization's benefit. If he'd refused, they would have turn him over to the several governments that wanted him for his crimes—in addition to the crimes fabricated by the Dieci that would have him in prison for the rest of his life.

"I don't want to be indebted to them for the rest of my life, mate," Oliver had told Robert over one of their many online chat sessions.

In addition to Oliver, Robert made two other friends who were associated with the Dieci—Ivan and Erasmo. Ivan had worked security for one member, but after witnessing that member commit murder he'd tried to leave the organization. As with Robert, the Dieci threatened the life of someone he loved as a way of making him comply—his young son Anton back in Moscow.

As for Erasmo, he had once been a full-fledged member of the Dieci. He had a background working in Turkish intelligence and was almost as technically skilled as Oliver. Yet once he suspected their destructive plans, he threatened to go to the authorities with what he knew. They killed his partner in retaliation, and Erasmo had gone into hiding.

The three men formed a brotherhood, intent on taking down the Dieci from the inside. Robert knew he had to destroy the Dieci. Somehow. Adrian and Cora would never be safe as long as it was around.

They had just begun to work on their plan when he heard whispers of his daughter's name from higher ups in the Dieci. First, there was the Cleopatra discovery. And then, her activities in Russia, preventing a dangerous weapon from falling into the wrong hands.

But it was her recent discovery of the lost city of Atlantis that put her on a direct collision course with the Dieci. After taking down the Greek branch of the organization, she officially had a target on her back. Oliver warned him that his daughter was now on their radar; she was becoming more than just a nuisance, and they were planning to take her out of the picture.

It was this, and only this that had made Robert act. It accelerated the plans he'd already made. He'd taken a significant risk to leave the note for her in her apartment in DC, the note leading her to Venice.

Now, he looked at his daughter's ashen face, forcing himself back to the present. As expected, she looked thoroughly shaken by all that he had told her.

"Everything I've done for the past decade has been for you and your mother, sweetheart," he murmured, giving her an imploring look. "And now I'm going to end this. All of it."

CHAPTER 8

Present Day
Dubrovnik, Croatia
10:07 PM

Adrian took a shuddering breath, reeling from both the fact that her father was alive, and everything he'd just told her.

"I know that all of this is a lot to learn, but there's more," her father continued, after a tense beat. "Saving your life was the main reason I approached you, but there's also something else. The Dieci are planning something. You foiled what their Greek branch was planning with Atlantis, but they have a plan B. I don't know what it is. They're keeping it under tight wraps. Ollie has only been able to tell me scant details. He thinks it may be another weapon—something that can cause mass casualties. Their code word for it is key."

"Is that why you mentioned a key? In the note you left for me at my apartment?" Adrian asked, recalling the letter that had started this all, that had led to Venice in the first place. *The key you seek lies within the floating city.*

"Indeed. I've had the word 'key' on the brain ever since I learned it was their code word for this weapon. The note I left you . . . it was very much like the scavenger hunt notes I used to leave for you on your birthday," Robert added quietly.

Adrian's throat tightened with emotion. All throughout her childhood and teen years, her father would leave her coded letters and ciphers to solve in order to find her birthday presents. Adrian had loved the practice, often looking forward to solving the puzzles more than her actual presents.

Her father held her gaze for a moment, locked in this shared memory, before clearing his throat and looking away. "I do know that whatever they're planning to do is linked to Venice—and also here, in Dubrovnik. Ollie told me they've found something here that will help them. He just doesn't know exactly what it is."

Adrian thought of this organization, recalling the Atlantis case and the weapon buried with Atlantis that the ancient secret society, Archaia Sofia, was looking for, which turned out to be Greek fire.

Their goal was to cause destruction in the form of mass casualties to begin anew. She'd thought—

hoped—that with the leader's death and the prosecution of many of its other members, that particular threat was over. She hadn't considered the possibility of other branches linked to Archaia Sofia . . . active ones. But the staging of suicides was familiar from what she knew of Archaia Sofia. It was their modus operandi and how they committed high-profile murders without detection. Dread coiled around her spine at the thought.

"I wanted to talk to you in Venice, but they had people on the ground there, so I had to get you away," her father was saying, forcing her back to the present.

"Was that you? Outside of our hotel in Venice?" Adrian asked, recalling the familiar-looking man she'd seen.

"Yes. I paid a young man to bump into you and give you that flyer. I considered approaching you directly, but it was too risky," her father confessed. "Now that you know what's going on, I want you—and your mother—to go into hiding."

Worry filled her at the mention of her mother. Her mother had sent her a text earlier, but Adrian hadn't yet responded.

"I have someone on your mother—he has a background in security and I trust him," Robert reassured her. "I'm going to do what I can to stop them and finally take them down. But I'll feel better knowing you and your mother are safe."

Nick let out a snort of disbelief. "You want

Adrian to go into hiding? You really don't know your daughter."

"I know how capable you are," Robert said, giving her another imploring look. "But these people want you dead. I know what they're capable of, I've seen it firsthand. It's best if—"

"No," Adrian snapped. "I agree with you about getting Mom to safety, but everything you just described . . . this is what I do. It's why I rejoined the bureau. I'm not going to run and hide. You're the one who needs to go into hiding. I can contact my boss at the bureau, have them—"

"No," Robert said emphatically. "I'll be dead before I get on the plane to wherever they try to hide me. I don't care about my life—I care about you, your mother, and the millions of people these monsters are intent on slaughtering. I'm not going anywhere until I stop them."

"I'm a federal agent. I'm trained. I can—"

"I've been working for this organization for years," Robert returned sharply. "I know it inside and out. I'm the one who—"

"As someone who knows how ingrained the stubbornness gene is in the West line," Nick interrupted, holding up his hands, "I'm going to save us all a lot of time. We're going to work together on this. No one, except for Adrian's mother, is going into hiding."

Adrian glared at her father, a glare which Robert returned. But she knew Nick was right. As much as she wanted to get her father out of harm's way, it was probably for the best that they work together.

"Fine," she said through gritted teeth. "Now—about Mom. Who is this person you have on her? Where is he going to take her?"

"His name is Ivan Vasiliev. He works security for the organization, but they're making him work for them, the same as me, using his son's life as an incentive. He's a good man. I told him not to tell me where he's taking her, just to get her out of Alexandria. "

Adrian closed her eyes, her mind whirling, but made herself focus. "We need to know more about this other branch of Archaia Sofia. You say they call themselves the Dieci?"

"Yes," her father confirmed. "At first, I only reported to the woman who took me captive—I only knew her as Valentina. If it wasn't her, it was one of her underlings, and I never worked under the same person more than once. I lived mostly in Mestre, on the outskirts of Venice, in various apartments paid for by the Dieci. They moved me every year or so. Whenever I traveled, one or two of their men always accompanied me to prevent any escape attempt. I was watched very closely, even my internet usage was monitored. It was only through Ollie setting me up with a private VPN that I was able to connect and talk to him, Ivan and Erasmo. Other than that . . . I don't know much about their inner workings. They were careful and secretive."

"We can reach out to Athena Karras for more

information," Nick added. She and Nick had worked with Athena, then a lieutenant constable with the Hellenic Police, during their time on the Atlantis case. She had since been promoted to sergeant and was now in charge of apprehending the remaining members of Archaia Sofia.

Adrian nodded her agreement. "And we need to find out what this organization found here in Dubrovnik. Does your contact—Oliver—have any more specific information about what they could be looking for?" she asked her father.

"He didn't know any more than what I told you," Robert said with a sigh of frustration. "Ever since I learned that whatever they're looking for is centered on Venice, I've been reading up on the city's history. One thing I noticed is Dubrovnik's historical ties to Venice. Given its location, it was both enemy and friend to Venice at various points in history. There were the Croatian Venetian Wars, where they fought for territory of the Adriatic. And then during the thirteenth century, it was ruled by Venice for over a century. They were also linked by trade."

"There must be something else . . . some recent find that links the two. Maybe something that hasn't been leaked to the press yet," Adrian said slowly. "I have contacts I can ask."

"You need to be incredibly discreet," Robert warned. "These people have eyes everywhere."

Alexandria, Virginia
4:57 PM

Cora flexed her cuffed hands, her pulse racing with panic.

She was seated in the passenger's side of an old beat up Chevy driven by her abductor, a large and foreboding man who continually cast tense gazes at the rearview mirror as he sped through the streets. She was shaking and terrified, blinking back tears.

Right after clamping his hand over her mouth, he'd dragged her out of the back door of her home, her struggles useless as she fought against his overwhelming strength.

As soon as they'd gotten to his car, parked in the alley behind her home, he'd loosened his grip to unlock the door. Cora had twisted her body in his grasp, opening her mouth to scream, but stiffened when she felt the sharp barrel of a gun against her spine.

"I would not do that," he'd muttered in a heavy Russian accent.

Now, as they got further and further away from her house, some of the tension seemed to dissipate from his large frame. Looking around, he pulled over and parked on an empty side street. He turned to face her, his expression grave.

"I am going to uncuff you. Sorry I had to, but we had no time. The men entering your house would have killed us. I will explain more, but I need your promise that you will not scream or run."

"I—I won't," Cora lied. She was going to strike him in the groin, just as Adrian had taught her, then run and scream like her life depended on it.

He must have seen the lie in her eyes, because he sighed. "I need you listen very closely to me," he said, after a lengthy pause. "I know your husband."

Cora stared at him in disbelief, her fear replaced by rage. "My husband is dead. How dare you—"

"While you were still dating, your husband made up a secret language, something that only the two of you understood. You used it more in the years before Adrian was born, but you both never forgot. The first words in this language that he spoke to you were, '*U Emet Dasre*'. He told me you would know what that meant."

Cora stiffened, looking at him in shocked disbelief. No one else but she and Robert knew about their secret language, which Robert had jokingly called 'RobertandCoraLang'. She clearly recalled the first words in the language he'd uttered to her. *U Emet Dasre.*

I love you always.

A fresh wave of tears pricked her eyes. She was still so shaken by his words that she made no attempt to flee as he reached out to uncuff her. Cora rubbed at her wrists once they were free, reeling.

"He sent me here because you are in danger. I got there just in time—had I been five minutes later, you would not be breathing now."

"I—I'm not going to take your word for it," she said finally. She wanted what he told her to be true, desperately. But she needed proof. "If my husband is alive, I want to speak to him."

CHAPTER 9

Dubrovnik, Croatia
10:31 PM

From the screen on Adrian's laptop, Sergeant Athena Karras stared at them in stunned silence.

"Another branch of Archaia Sophia," she said finally, shaking her head in disbelief. "I should have known."

Adrian met her gaze, offering Athena a grim nod. After Adrian had sent an email to her contacts requesting information on any recent archaeological finds in Dubrovnik, she and Nick had contacted Athena, filling her in on what they'd learned from Adrian's father.

"I'm sorry we had to spring this on you, given how busy I know you must be," Adrian said. "But according to our source, this other branch is actively seeking another weapon, and they may be close to finding it."

Adrian had opted to leave out her father's part in all this, simply referring to him as their 'source'. While she trusted Athena, she knew her father was wary of too many people knowing of his status.

"What have you learned from other members you've apprehended?" Nick asked Athena.

"Well, many were unaware of Stephanos' true plans. They just wanted the riches associated with Atlantis. No one I've interviewed mentioned any other current branch, just the one centered in Athens, though there are members all over the world."

"What about Archaia Sophia's history?" Adrian pressed. "Were there other branches in the past?"

"It was once a single organization centered in Athens during the Greco-Roman era that focused on 'seeking wisdom'. Over time, it was assumed that it did splinter into branches in other places, but the members I've interviewed assumed those other branches have long since died out."

Adrian nodded slowly, thinking of the other secret societies she'd encountered since returning to the bureau. It seemed common for them to splinter into different groups over time, akin to modern day terror cells. She could imagine a splinter group forming in Venice, especially at the height of the republic's power.

"If any of the people you've interviewed know

of members living in Venice, that could be a start," Adrian said.

"Will do. And I'll see what else I can find out," Athena said.

They shared goodbyes and logged off the video call. Adrian turned to Nick, who looked as frustrated as she felt. She'd hoped that Athena would have more information, but she'd been just as flummoxed as they were.

Adrian still couldn't quite believe that her father was just in the other room, living and breathing. After his disappearance and presumed death, he had become something abstract, a hazy memory that she'd struggled to hold on to. She had desperately wanted her father to be alive, of course, and knew her mother had the same hope, but she'd forced herself to be practical. She'd worked many missing persons cases during her time with the bureau and knew that after a certain amount of time, the chances of a missing person being found alive was slim to none. Still, the hope had prevailed, a tiny part of her believing that, until they found a body, her father could still be alive.

And he was.

She wished she had time to fully process all that he'd told her, but she had to focus on stopping this organization that was actively seeking a weapon. They needed to be stopped—yesterday.

Her phone suddenly chimed with an email notification, and she glanced down at it. Relief chased away her frustration, and she looked up at Nick with a grin.

"What?" he asked.

"We have a lead."

IN THE NEXT ROOM, Robert took in his wife's face on the screen of his phone. Like Adrian, he had caught glimpses of her in images over the years, but there was nothing like seeing her live, staring at him directly. Her dark brown wavy hair was now streaked with gray, and fine lines had appeared around her hazel eyes, which were now filled with an age-worn wisdom. She was even more beautiful than he remembered; age had only enhanced her loveliness. His Cora.

As soon as he'd seen the number of the incoming call on his phone, he knew it was Ivan. His heart pounded with fear as he'd answered, terrified that something had gone wrong. He'd listened with unease as Ivan told him about rescuing Cora from her home before men sent from the Dieci could get to her.

"Do not worry. She is safe now. She wants to speak to you," Ivan said, before handing over the phone to Cora.

Robert and Cora sat in silence for a few moments, just taking each other in. It wasn't until Cora's eyes moved to a point behind him that he turned; Adrian and Nick were entering the room.

Her daughter's entrance seemed to break the spell Cora was under, and when she finally spoke, her words were directed at Adrian.

"Adrian," Cora said, her eyes again straying to Robert, as if he were a ghost that would disappear at any moment. "How—how is this possible?"

Robert chose to answer before his daughter could respond. "It's a long story, Cora, and one I intend to tell you in person. But right now, you're in a lot of danger. My friend is there to get you somewhere safe."

Adrian stepped forward, leaning in closer to the screen. She gave her mother a comforting smile. "I know this is a lot to take in, but he's right. I just found out he's still alive myself. We can explain more once you're somewhere safe."

Cora's face drained of even more color. "But what about you? Are you—"

"You know I'm used to this," Adrian gently interrupted. "This is my job. But I need to know you're safe in order to do it."

Cora swallowed, but nodded, her gaze turning back to Robert.

"I can't wait to see you in person when you're truly safe," he said. "I love you, Cora. You have no idea how much I've missed you both. There's so much more I want to say . . . so much I *will* say." He reached out and touched the image of her face on the screen. Cora closed her eyes, taking a shuddering breath, as if he'd actually touched her. "You need to go with Ivan and trust him. He will keep you safe. OK?"

"OK," Cora murmured. Her eyes strayed to Adrian. "I love you."

"Thank you, Ivan," Robert said gruffly when his friend's face appeared on the screen after Cora reluctantly handed him the phone.

Ivan merely nodded; he was a man of few words. "I will send an encrypted message once we are out of the DC area," he said, before ending the call.

Robert stared at his phone, as if willing the image of his wife's face to appear again. It wasn't until he felt his daughter's hand on his shoulder that he glanced up. She looked more guarded than she had with her mother, but offered him the same comforting smile.

"She's in shock right now. You have no idea how much she's missed you," Adrian said.

Now that the elation over seeing his wife had faded, anger flared in his gut. He'd wanted to be reunited with his wife and daughter when he knew they were safe, not under these circumstances. But the Dieci had forced his hand.

He filled Adrian and Nick in on what Ivan had told him about the men that had broken into Cora's home. Fear filled him at what would have happened had Ivan not gotten there in time. His daughter paled, and he imagined she was thinking the same thing.

"These men . . . I assume they work for the

Dieci? How did they get to her so fast?" Adrian asked, after a fraught pause.

"They must know already that I've gone AWOL. I tried my best to cover my tracks, but—" he shook his head, more frustration filling him.

"We need to get ahead of them," Adrian said. "And we will. I heard from one of my contacts, Elias Mandreou. A local curator here in Dubrovnik, Lucija Novak, told him there was a coded letter found in a home in Old Town that once belonged to a Venetian merchant. The letter dates from the twelfth century."

"It's now missing," Nick added.

Robert considered this. The missing letter could have nothing to do with what the Dieci was looking for here in Dubrovnik, but his gut told him otherwise. Stealing historical documents was a common practice for them; he'd lost count of how many such documents they'd made him decipher over the years.

"We need to find that letter—or find out what was in it," he said.

His daughter and Nick exchanged a look. He noticed that they did this often, as if there were some invisible link that joined them.

"We know just where to start," Nick said.

CHAPTER 10

Vrânceanu Institute of Historical Archaeology
Bucharest, Romania
10:47 PM

Polina was barely paying attention to the celebratory hubbub around her. The institute's employees were having a small late-night party in the cafeteria, celebrating a recent archaeological find that the institute would be in charge of handling. It was a mass grave beneath the ruins of an ancient Dacian fortress on the outskirts of the city. The institute was often competing with the University of Bucharest for spearheading archaeological digs and analyses, so this was significant for them.

Polina held a glass of țuică, Romania's national celebratory drink, a sour cherry brandy that she usually enjoyed, but she had yet to take a sip. And she would usually be just as excited as her colleagues. As someone who studied old bones, findings of mass graves were exciting for her. All she could think about, however, were the odd samples she'd studied earlier, and her boss' even odder reaction. Polina was scanning the room for Mikhail or Florin, determined to get more information.

Earlier that day, she'd grudgingly sent over her data to Florin. She'd watched as Mikhail pulled Florin aside before they'd both abruptly left the office. She'd continued to perform her other tasks, writing a report on findings from the previous week and prepping for review of the samples she was to look over next, her eyes continually straying to Mikhail's office, but he didn't return for the rest of the day. Neither had Florin. Her unease had continued to rise, no matter how much she tried to push it aside.

Polina stiffened as she spotted Florin enter the cafeteria, smiling as a colleague handed him a glass of țuică. She hurried toward him, but a lab assistant she was friendly with, Elisabeta, intercepted her.

"I was in the field when they made the find . . . I can't believe how exciting it was. I hear we're going to get even more funding now," Elisabeta gushed.

Polina nodded and offered a smile, keeping her gaze trained on Florin. She continued to murmur polite responses until she was finally able to excuse herself, making a beeline toward Florin.

He spotted her coming toward him, freezing

before abruptly turning to leave. Polina was so surprised by this that she momentarily halted in her tracks. Usually, Florin would use what happened today as an opportunity to lord his superiority over her. His avoiding her just confirmed that something odd was going on here.

She hurried after him, weaving around the sea of her colleague's bodies until she exited the cafeteria and reached the corridor Florin had disappeared into. She looked up and down the corridor, spotting his retreating figure hurrying toward the exit.

Taking off after him at a jog, she reached him just as he reached the doors. "Florin—I wanted to ask you about the samples—"

"I have to go," he said shortly, not looking at her.

"What did you find?" she pressed. "Were the samples contaminated? Was—"

"There was nothing. You must have made a mistake. All the pathogens had the same genetic material."

Polina frowned. She knew what she saw in the samples. Florin was lying to her. "Florin—"

Florin roughly grabbed her arm, his expression tense. "Just forget about the samples, OK? They're no longer your concern."

There were traces of fear—and worry—in his eyes. Before she could press, he hurried out the exit, leaving a stunned Polina in his wake.

Venice, Italy
10:58 PM

VITTORIA MADE her way down the long corridor of her Venetian home that overlooked the Grand Canal. A sense of peace often descended over her whenever she spent time in the palatial home she'd inherited from her mother, with its wood paneled floors and walls filled with her mother's collection of paintings, its floor-to-ceiling windows with views of the Grand Canal.

But not today. Her body was tense, every sense on high alert.

Her bodyguard Isabella stood outside the drawing room, and Vittoria gave her a nod as she entered. The windows gave her a perfect view of the moon hovering over the canal; it seemed particularly bright tonight, illuminating the dark waters of the lagoon and casting the old buildings that lined it in an ethereal glow.

The five men and one other woman who were gathered turned to face her, their expressions hard. They were some of the other leaders of the Dieci, the only ones who could come to her on such short notice. Despite their stony expressions, Vittoria gave them a gracious smile, ignoring the turbulent emotions that were swirling inside her.

"Thank you for meeting with me on such short

notice," she said, pouring herself a glass of lemon water that the housekeeper had left on the long central table. "We have tracked Adrian West and her partner to Dubrovnik, and we believe her father may be with them. Rest assured, the person I have on them is reliable. West and her father's involvement can only mean that we're on the right track."

"Or," said Paolo Marini, his tone icy. He was one of the younger members of the Dieci, only in his late twenties, and had inherited his position from his father. As far as Vittoria was concerned, he had no place in the Dieci, much less as one of its leaders. He was ignorant to the old society's ways and petulant. Paolo didn't truly believe in the cause, he just wanted power. He glowered at her as he continued, "They already know everything, and the plan has been compromised."

"They won't find what they're looking for in Dubrovnik, it's been taken care of," Vittoria said cooly. "And they will be taken care of as well. Robert West will face consequences for his betrayal."

"How is everything else proceeding?" Matteo Bianchi, an austere man in his fifties, asked. He had been close with her mother, yet still did not take her seriously.

"My lab in Geneva is still carrying out tests, and so far, the results look promising. The plan is proceeding well. Nothing has changed."

"I hope so," Paolo said tersely. "After

Stephanos' failure with Atlantis, everyone is on edge."

She stiffened at the mention of Stephanos, a tempestuous leader of the Greek branch of Archaia Sofia who had found Atlantis, only to foolishly die in the process and lead the authorities right to it.

"I'm not Stephanos," she snapped. "He was hot-headed and a fool. I know how to keep a level head. My mother taught me well."

She held Paolo's gaze, daring him to challenge her.

Her mother had been one of the few female leaders of the Dieci. Everyone she knew had revered Valentina Trivisana for her ruthlessness—and her effectiveness. Her father had only loosely been a member, and he'd died of natural causes when she was still a child. It was her mother who had helped take the Dieci from an aging, largely dormant organization to a powerful force; she was the one who had discovered the reference to the 'key' in their archives and spearheaded the plans Vittoria was now continuing, from setting up and funding the lab in Geneva to recruiting assets all around the world to help further their plans—including Robert West, Adrian West's father. Vittoria had no doubt that her mother would still be a powerful force in the Dieci had a fatal heart attack not struck her down a couple of years ago, after which Vittoria had taken her place.

The mention of her mother seemed to placate the members, and the meeting concluded after she answered more of their questions about how their plans were proceeding. They all seemed satisfied by her answers—except for Paolo, who glowered at her throughout the remainder of the meeting.

After they left, Vittoria watched from the window as another member of her security team, Bernardo, guided them to the private motorboat waiting by the docks in front of her home that would transport them down the canal and back to the airport.

Irritation rippled through her as she recalled their doubts, but she reminded herself it would take time for them to fully accept her capabilities. She had only officially joined the Dieci several years ago, while some of the others had been members for decades. Though there were hundreds of members of the organization, there were only ten leaders, including her. Their full official name was *Il Consiglio dei Dieci*, the Council of Ten, based on the Venetian council that once ran the republic at the height of its power. The Dieci had its origins in ancient Rome as part of Archaia Sofia, before splintering off into its own branch after Roman refugees fled to the Venetian lagoons as the old empire fell. The Dieci had operated in the shadows of Venice's then official Council of Ten, focused on its purpose of the 'ancient wisdom' . . . destruction for renewal.

It was hard to believe that Vittoria had once disagreed with everything the Dieci stood for, causing a long estrangement between her and her mother . . . . until she herself had lost everything.

The motorboat roared away, and she turned to leave the drawing room, telling Isabella she needed some privacy. Isabella dutifully left her alone, heading downstairs as Vittoria made her way to the study, drawn as always to a photograph she kept there, one she couldn't bring herself to put away.

In the photo, her husband and son, Ben and Massimo, were laughing as they held onto each other, the Cannaregio Canal behind them. She could remember that day like it was yesterday.

It had been a lovely spring day. She and Ben had taken Massimo to get gelato before they all went to the island of Murano, where their son watched the glassblowers work, his dark eyes wide with wonder. Though it had been years since she'd lost them, the grief was sudden—sharp and swift—piercing her like the tip of a sharp blade. She clutched the side of the desk, steeling her breaths, fighting against the pain.

Closing her eyes, she shoved the photo down and turned away from it, shutting out the dark memories. She focused on the only thing that numbed the pain; the thing that would bring everything to fruition. It would prevent tragedies like Ben and Massimo's deaths from ever happening again.

The key.

Dubrovnik, Croatia

11:02 PM

Adrian, Nick and her father crept through the cobblestoned back alley that led to Lucija Novak's home in Old Town. Like many dwellings in this neighborhood, it was a narrow two-story stone house, nestled between other similar homes that were built into the patchwork of winding streets. The lights of Lucija's home were out, and no one appeared to be inside.

They'd tried to reach Lucija by phone and email, but there was no response. She knew it wasn't likely they'd get a response at this hour, but this was urgent and they didn't want to risk waiting until morning. Still, it wasn't a good sign that they couldn't reach her, and unease filled Adrian's gut.

They stopped several yards away from the back door. She and Nick regarded it warily, readying their weapons. Given their past experiences, they weren't taking any chances. Adrian turned to her father.

"Stay behind us," she said firmly.

Robert obliged, falling behind as they approached the back door. Adrian knocked several times, unsurprised that there was no answer. Still, alarm spiked in her belly, and she locked eyes with Nick.

"Time for Plan B," he said, and using his weapon, he shattered the narrow glass window next to the back door.

Adrian held her breath, waiting to see if they

had attracted a neighbor or stray tourist's attention, but there was only silence. Nick reached in through the window and opened the back door.

As soon as they entered the kitchen, Adrian knew that Lucija was long gone. Everything was bare; it looked as if someone had left in a hurry.

Adrian turned to face her father and Nick.

"We should—" she began, but her father's eyes suddenly widened in alarm. He leapt forward, tackling her to the ground, just as bullets tore into the kitchen.

CHAPTER 11

*A*drian rolled out from beneath her father, shouting at him to stay down. The shots had stopped—for now.

She looked over at Nick, who was already moving at a crouch toward the doorway that led from the kitchen to the living room, his weapon at his side. Adrian gestured to her father for him to hide. He hesitated for a moment before obliging her, tucking himself away behind a massive cabinet on the far side of the kitchen. Only then did she join Nick by the doorway, crouched low.

The shooter was silent. Too silent. Adrian remained still, holding her breath. She looked at Nick, and just as they were about to spring from their hiding places—

The shooter fired several more shots into the kitchen, this time at closer range, barely missing her father's hiding place. Fury coursed through her, and ignoring Nick's warning shout, she leapt up from her crouch and charged into the next room, raising her weapon to fire.

A hulking man with cold, dark eyes stood there, his pistol raised, but he dove to the floor as she fired at him. On the floor, he twisted his large body, raising his weapon, firing off two more shots. Adrian dodged and returned fire, but he raced out of the living room.

Adrian and Nick dashed after him, but the shooter was ready, and as soon as they entered the next room, he barreled toward them, knocking Nick to the floor. He raised his weapon again, but Adrian lunged forward, taking him out at his knees and sending him crashing to the floor. Nick rolled over and used all of his strength to pin the man to the ground as Adrian rolled away. But to her horror, the shooter quickly overpowered Nick with a fierce growl, pressing his weapon to the side of his head—

Adrian aimed and fired at the shooter's chest. He slumped forward, dead. She hurried forward to help Nick out from under him.

"You OK?" she asked.

"Alive, thanks to you," Nick replied, his breathing labored as she helped him to his feet.

They looked down at the shooter, and together, they rolled him over, searching him for identification or a phone, but there was nothing on him. Adrian let out a frustrated curse. She shouldn't have killed him, but instinct had taken over the moment he'd pressed his gun to the head of the man she loved.

Her father entered the room, his face pale. He looked down at the shooter, swallowing.

"Do you recognize him?" Adrian asked.

Robert studied him for a long moment before shaking his head. Adrian straightened, snapping a photo of the shooter's face. Hopefully, the task force could find something on him through facial recognition.

The sound of car tires screeching up to the house made them both look up. Panic lodged in Adrian's throat as Nick moved to the window, peeking out, his expression turning grim.

"It looks like our friend here has backup. We have to get the hell out of here."

MOMENTS LATER, Adrian, Nick and her father were racing down the alley away from Lucija's house, taking back streets until they were a considerable distance away. Only then did they slow their pace and cut out onto a main road, blending in with a drunken group of tourists who were making their way to one of Dubrovnik's many seaside restaurants and bars.

Adrian glanced over at her father, who didn't seem that winded. Her father's physical prowess impressed her; he'd held his own with Adrian and Nick as they'd ran. Her father had never been significantly overweight or noticeably out of shape, but he had just been a mostly sedentary college professor. She noticed that he'd become leaner since his disappearance, with more muscle. Adrian recalled that he'd even hesitated when she told him to stay back during their encounter with the shooter . . . as if he'd considered helping.

Seeming to read her mind, her father gave her a rueful grin. "A side effect of being the hostage of an international criminal secret society . . . you get in better shape. Ivan helped me with building muscle and stamina. I knew I'd need it one day when I take these bastards down." He looked around, his expression turning serious as he lowered his voice. "We can't go back to the hotel."

"Agreed," Nick said. "We could reach out to the task force. They can help us find a safe house."

"No," Robert said immediately. "I don't trust the authorities. We do need to get out of the city, though. I know where we can go."

CHAPTER 12

Čibača, Croatia
1:15 AM

Čibača was a quaint seaside village located southeast of Dubrovnik. Once there, her father drove to the edge of the village, parking in front of a modest, one-story, Mediterranean-style home nestled high on a bluff, just steps from the Adriatic.

Robert told them it belonged to Oliver, one of his friends in the Dieci. He assured them that Oliver had taken many steps to ensure it was completely off the radar. There was even a security system with cameras mounted on top of the house, monitoring the road that led to it.

"I've only been here a handful of times over the years, but each time it's given me a sense of peace," he said, glancing around the living room with a small smile tugging at his lips.

Adrian looked at him, mixed emotions coursing through her. How many times had her father come here for a relaxing beach vacation while she and her mother grieved? She told herself that hadn't been the situation at all, but she couldn't quell the bitterness that filled her at the thought.

"They're still following us," Adrian said, forcing her mind back to the present. "How else would they know we'd be at Lucija's house?"

"Or they could have been watching the house," Robert said grimly.

"Either way, this proves the Dieci was involved with the stolen letter," Nick added.

"If Lucija didn't get to safety in time, they've killed her for what she knows," Robert said bluntly. "I know how they operate. I'm going to reach out to Ollie and see if he can get access to the letter—there may be a digital version stored somewhere. But for now . . . we all need rest."

Robert led Adrian and Nick to a guest room, his gaze lingering on Adrian before leaving them.

Adrian watched him go, feeling an almost childlike need to not let him out of her sight. She silently chided herself for feeling this way. She was a grown woman in her thirties . . . but the feeling persisted.

"I sent Vince the photo we took of the shooter for him to run through facial recognition. I asked him to keep it under wraps and didn't tell him what it was for, but I know he's curious."

"Good. Thanks," Adrian said, still distracted.

Nick studied her for a moment before stepping forward, wrapping his arms around her and pulling her close.

"You haven't told me how you feel," he said quietly, "about your father being alive."

"There's a lot of feelings right now. I'm overwhelmed. Relieved. Happy. In disbelief. I'm . . . a little angry, too. Not at him—I know he did this to protect us. But I've been grieving for a decade, Nick. So has my mother. And to know that he was alive, the whole time, a captive . . . " Tears pricked at her eyes, and she blinked them back.

Nick pressed a kiss to her forehead. "I know. It's a lot. You're going to feel what you're going to feel. It's just going to take time for this all to sink in."

Adrian leaned into the comfort of Nick's embrace, allowing determination to replace her tumult of emotions as she thought about the encounter with the shooter at Lucija's home. The encounter had proven just how urgent their mission was. And as she thought of them holding her father captive, she was even more determined to stop the Dieci from carrying out their deadly goal.

CHAPTER 13

Dulles, Virginia
7:27 PM

"You can talk to him one more time. Any more—too much risk," Ivan snapped, his glower menacing.

Cora glowered right back. With his large frame, Ivan was intimidating, and he'd scared the hell out of her the first time she'd seen him. But ever since her husband's reassurances, and the small fact of him saving her life, she was feeling more at ease around him—and that included standing up to him.

After the phone call with Robert and her daughter, Ivan had driven them to a nondescript motel just outside of Washington Dulles airport. He wouldn't tell her where they were going, just somewhere safe, and that they'd be leaving early the next morning. At his suggestion, she'd called into the accounting firm where she worked, telling her boss she was having a family emergency and she'd be away for at least a couple of weeks.

"Is it your daughter?" Phil, her boss, had asked with concern. "Is everything all right?"

Ever since Adrian's discovery of Cleopatra's tomb months ago, her daughter had become somewhat of a celebrity around the office; her coworkers were all well aware of her work with the bureau. It came as no surprise that they'd assume any family emergency had to do with Adrian.

Still, a ripple of annoyance coursed through Cora at his prying, even though he was somewhat correct. *Actually, no, Phil. My daughter is pretty much always in lethal danger, which is a fun thing for a mother to get used to. It's actually my dead husband, who is in fact alive, just, you know, an evil secret society has held him captive for the past decade.*

After assuring Phil that her daughter was fine and getting off the phone before he could pry further, she'd repeatedly demanded to speak to Robert again. At first Ivan had refused, telling her it was too risky. But Cora was willing to take the risk. She'd lost count of how many times she'd let herself hope that Robert was still alive, even as she put on a brave front for her daughter and concerned friends. Even after she'd made herself hold a funeral for him. She *needed* to see his face again and hear his voice. To convince herself this wasn't just some vivid dream, and she'd awaken to learn that he was, in fact, still gone.

Ivan finally relented, muttering something in Russian that she assumed wasn't flattering. She didn't care. As long as she could speak to her husband again.

Ivan took out his phone and dialed a number. He handed it to her before leaving the room to give her privacy.

Robert answered almost immediately, looking at her with alarm. "Cora, what is it? Are you OK? Where's Ivan?"

"Everything's fine. I browbeat him into letting me speak to you again."

Robert's face relaxed, and he smiled. Cora returned his smile, taking in his features, the ones she had committed to memory. The first time she'd spoken to him, she'd been too shocked to truly take him in, but now she allowed herself to. He had aged, fine lines and wrinkles where they weren't before, and there was now a hardness to him. Still, he was the most handsome man she'd ever seen, just as handsome as he was when he was just a graduate student when they'd first met.

"You're more beautiful than ever, coral," he said, reverting to the nickname he'd given her when they first started dating, and another rush of emotions flowed through her. She lifted her hand to trace his features, longing to see and touch him for real.

"I know we don't have long to talk," she said. "And I know you want to tell me everything in person. But I need to know where you've been for the past decade."

She feared he'd resist, but he told her about his capture from the airport in Istanbul, some of the work he'd done for the Dieci over the years, keeping track of her and Adrian, and finally what had made him come out of hiding—the threat to Adrian's life, which caused a spiral of fear to spread throughout her belly.

Cora listened intently to every word. She could tell he had condensed his tale, and that over time there would be far, far more details. By the haunted look in his eyes, his years away had been harrowing. When he fell silent, he gazed at her for a long moment.

"How do you feel?" he asked.

"Everything," Cora said, her eyes welling up with tears. "I feel—everything."

"I did this for our daughter. For you. Nothing less than your lives would have kept me away," he said fervently. "Our little girl is something else."

"She certainly is," Cora said, pride swelling in her chest. "But don't ever call her 'little girl' to her face."

"Oh, I won't," Robert said with a chuckle, before his expression turned serious. "When they threatened her—" His voice broke, and a look of fierce protectiveness arose in his expression, an emotion Cora recognized. She knew in that moment that she would have done the same thing in his position.

"I know," Cora said. "Robert . . . I understand." Anger rose in her at the thought of the monsters who had taken Robert, who had threatened their daughter's life. She expelled a breath. "Tell me more about this—organization. Ivan hasn't told me much."

"I will," Robert said grimly. "*After* I stop them and take them down. I want to talk to you for hours, days, weeks . . . but Ivan is right. We've been careful with these phones, but it's too risky for us to keep talking. We've been on this line for too long. Before I go—" he hedged, suddenly looking bashful. "I know it's been a very long time, and Adrian didn't mention anything, but if there's someone—someone in your life that you care about—"

"Robert," she interrupted, "some part of me must have always known you were still out there. There is no one else. There never will be anyone but you."

Relief softened his features, and he gave her another one of his heart-stopping smiles. "Coral," he murmured. "My Coral."

"You come home to me," she said firmly. "And I know Adrian is as tough as nails, but keep our girl safe."

Čibača, Croatia
8:03 AM

"Oliver was able to dig into Lucija's bank records. Before she went missing, not long after the discovery of the letter, she made several trips to a safe deposit box at a bank in Dubrovnik," Robert said.

Adrian and Nick sat at the kitchen table, where Robert had sat them down with two cups of coffee as soon as they'd emerged from the guest room, telling them he had news.

Adrian had hoped it was positive news; they'd woken to a text from Vince who had already run the shooter's face through facial recognition, but nothing came up. He'd not so subtly pressed for more information; Nick hadn't given him any. Adrian knew they'd have to eventually loop the task force in on all of this, but it would take some convincing her father, who was wary of law enforcement.

Now, Adrian took a sip of her coffee, wincing at its strength, her thoughts racing. "Then we need to get access to it."

"It'll be tricky, but I think we can do it. And that's where you come in," her father replied.

Adrian regarded him with a puzzled look. Grinning, Robert slid an identification card toward her. "Ollie sent me this to print out. You're going to use it to access her safe deposit box," Robert said.

As Adrian studied the photo, she understood. Lucija bore a striking resemblance to Adrian. If she tucked her hair away, and with the clever use of makeup and glasses, she could pass for the other woman.

"And the Dieci don't know about this bank account?" Nick asked.

"Lucija's account hasn't been touched since before she went missing, according to Ollie. The account is also under her married name, and she's now divorced, so that could be how they missed it."

They quickly came up with a plan, after which Nick politely excused himself to use the shower. Adrian shot him a look; she knew he was leaving on purpose to give her and her father some time alone. Nick returned her look with a grin as he left the kitchen.

Adrian drained her coffee, avoiding her father's eyes, and abruptly stood. "I should get prepared."

"I spoke to your mother last night. She's safe," he added, at her look of alarm. "She wanted to know about my years away, and I told her. She also made me promise to come home to her. Both of us."

Adrian met his eyes. There was so much she wanted to say, but she settled on simplicity . . . on their shared goal. "After we stop the Dieci, we'll keep that promise."

CHAPTER 14

Dubrovnik, Croatia
4:19 PM

Adrian entered the bank, keeping her expression neutral, though her pulse was fluttering faster than a hummingbird's wings.

She kept her head low to avoid the security camera as she approached the teller. Nick and Robert were waiting in a car a few blocks away, both of them making her promise she'd text them at any hint of trouble.

She had prepared all day to impersonate Lucija to access her safe deposit box. She'd tucked her hair away into a low bun and wore glasses, an ill-fitting blouse and slacks, all finds Nick had scoured from a local secondhand store. The biggest problem was her Croatian; it was unfortunately not one of the languages she was fluent in, but she did have a passing knowledge of it. Her knowledge of Russian helped, as they were both Slavic languages, but she was still nervous about pulling it off. She had practiced relevant phrases as much as she could and prayed the teller wouldn't find her accent too odd.

There were several other people being helped by tellers, so fortunately, all the focus wasn't on her. Adrian fixed a smile on her face as she approached the teller, handing her the fake identification card.

"Good afternoon. I just need to make a withdrawal from my safe deposit box," Adrian said in Croatian.

The teller studied her identification for such a long moment that Adrian held her breath, her body tense. To her relief, the teller handed it back to her with an amiable smile. "Of course, Miss Novak."

The teller handed her a key and gestured for Adrian to follow her. *So far, so good*, Adrian thought, trailing the teller from the main lobby and down a corridor to a locked room. The teller unlocked the door and gestured for her to enter, pointing out the safe deposit box in the far corner of the room before leaving her with a polite smile. Adrian watched her go, relief filling her. That was almost too easy.

Adrian made her way to Lucija's safe deposit box and unlocked it, filled with anticipation. She took out the box and opened it, even more relief flooding through her at what she found inside.

Inside, there were several pages of documents.

They appeared to be photocopies of a medieval letter. *The* letter.

She worked quickly, hastily taking photos of each section of the letter and texting them to Nick and her father before carefully sliding the hard copies into a document folder in her bag. She quickly replaced the box, and just as she turned to head out, she heard footsteps approaching the room.

Adrian froze. A security guard entered, his expression hard. The previously friendly teller hovered behind him with a suspicious frown.

"We need to ask you some questions, Miss Novak."

Adrian tried to look appropriately confused, though dread swirled through her veins. "Why? I don't understand."

"I need you to come with me," he repeated.

Adrian stared at him, her heart racing. What had gone wrong? But she didn't have time to ponder that now. She needed to act quickly.

She gave him a shaky nod, stepping forward. Taking a quick look behind him, she noticed the corridor was thankfully empty.

Adrian acted fast. She darted forward and removed the guard's gun from his holster in a quick move. He looked at her, startled, as Adrian raised the weapon, hitting him in the temple as hard as she could, causing him to crumple to the ground, still and unconscious.

The teller stumbled back, her eyes widening with fear, opening her mouth to scream. Adrian hated to do this, but she leveled the gun at the teller.

"I need your help getting out of this bank."

Moments later, Adrian was darting down one of the back streets that led away from the bank. Once she was a couple of streets away, she took off her heels and made a run for it, knowing that she didn't have long—the teller had likely already tripped the alarm. She had already dashed off a text to her father and Nick, telling them where to meet her.

She ignored the curious looks from locals and tourists alike as she raced barefoot down the narrow streets, ignoring the pain of the cobblestones digging into her bare feet, before turning onto the main thoroughfare of Lucarica Street.

Adrian picked up her pace, reaching the picturesque Luza Square, which featured the Dubrovnik Cathedral and the familiar facade of Saint Blaise's Church. She soon spotted her father's rental waiting at the edge of the square. She raced to the car and scrambled into the backseat, and her father immediately sped away.

Nick turned to look at her with concern. "You OK?"

Though the encounter with the security guard still rattled Adrian, she held up the document folder, giving him a smile.

"More than OK."

CHAPTER 15

Čibača, Croatia
8:23 PM

Adrian, Nick and her father stood over the dining table in the beach house, where they'd spread out the copies of the letter.

It had taken them some time to return from Dubrovnik, with Robert taking various side roads to ensure they weren't being followed. During the trip back, Adrian's frustration with herself increased; she must have done something to arouse the security guard's suspicion. She still wasn't certain why the security guard had pulled her aside. Adrian could only guess that she'd made some small mistake. Both Nick and her father reassured her she'd done well and all that mattered was that she'd gotten copies of the letter. Adrian was still uneasy. She suspected that the theft wouldn't go unnoticed, and someone from the Dieci would find out.

Adrian forced herself to concentrate on the letter, which consisted of roughly thirty lines written in Italian, along with fifty varying types of symbols.

"During its more powerful days, the Venetian Republic was filled to the brim with spies—from the Council of Ten down to the trade guilds. Merchants were especially useful as spies, given their access to foreign lands, both friendly and enemy. As a result, spies were good at creating codes and ciphers, especially in letters like these," Robert said.

"How the hell do we start decoding this?" Nick asked, studying the symbols with frustration.

"We need to categorize the symbols and look for a pattern," Robert said. "But first, let me translate."

Robert proceeded to read the letter out loud in English. It was a mundane letter in which the merchant discussed the quantities of salt that he'd successfully traded with the locals, addressed to a colleague of his in Venice.

"Wow. That was incredibly boring," Nick said, letting out an exaggerated yawn.

"I think that's the point," her father returned with a grin. "A letter like this is something a rival spy would overlook. The only giveaway that there's a hidden message here are the symbols. That's what we're going to focus on . . . and it might point to a hidden message beneath these otherwise boring details."

For the next several hours, Adrian, Nick and Robert set about decoding the letter. At first they made little progress, and Adrian feared they wouldn't be able to decode the letter alone.

But eventually, they were able to discern an emerging pattern, realizing that certain symbols coincided with particular letters—and full words.

They worked throughout the night, only stopping briefly to scarf down sandwiches her father hastily prepared for them. At some point, Nick took out a notepad and put together a list as they determined what each symbol likely meant.

Soon, they could decode the hidden message buried in the letter. They leaned over, taking in the words Nick had written on the legal pad.

> We will get revenge for what they have done. The Doctor in the Queen of Cities is creating a powerful poison that will strike them down.

~

Vrânceanu Institute of Historical Archaeology
Bucharest, Romania
11:58 PM

Polina left the records room, shutting it surreptitiously behind her. No one was here at this hour. The last employee had left just twenty minutes ago, she had made certain of it.

After her encounter with Florin last night, she had called, texted, and even emailed him. He had ignored all of her attempts to reach him. And Mikhail had conveniently not come into the office today.

So, she was resorting to sneaking around the lab to get access to the data on the Feodosia samples herself. Polina told herself that once she got confirmation that Florin was telling the truth, and she'd misidentified the genetic material, she would drop it. But she couldn't ignore her instincts that something else was going on. She'd had no luck so far, not finding any records of the samples anywhere . . . it was like they'd never been here.

Sighing, Polina made her way toward her lab, freezing when she heard male voices coming from the far end of the corridor. One of them was Mikhail's.

She frantically looked around for somewhere to hide. She scrambled into a nearby janitor's closet that was just opposite of Mikhail's office. Once inside, she held herself still, listening intently.

"The samples are taken care of," Mikhail was saying. "They won't be—"

His voice disappeared as he closed his office door, and Polina gritted her teeth in frustration. What did he mean the samples were taken care of? She had no doubt he was referring to the Feodosia samples. Had he destroyed them for some reason?

She was tempted to leave the closet to listen at Mikhail's door, but something told her to stay put. Instead, she listened to the muffled voices, trying to make out the words, but they were indiscernible.

Finally, after nearly an hour, she heard the door swing open.

The men walked by the closet. Now she could hear their words clearly.

And what she heard chilled her to the bone.

Of all the things she could have imagined . . . this was far worse.

CHAPTER 16

Čibača, Croatia
6:27 AM

"The Queen of Cities?" Nick echoed.

"A nickname given to one of the powerful cities of the ancient and medieval world," Robert said, looking up from the legal pad. "Then known as Constantinople... now Istanbul."

"And the reference to a doctor and poison," Adrian mused. "That could be the ancient weapon the Dieci is looking for."

"Yeah, but what type of weapon? It couldn't have been some sort of bioweapon. They didn't know about germs yet, much less how to weaponize them," Nick said, giving her a skeptical look.

"That's not true," Robert said, shaking his head. "True, germ theory was discovered much later, but doctors were very aware of infectiousness. There's a record of a Venetian doctor planning to use the 'quintessence' of plague against Venice's enemies during the Venetian Ottoman war—this was in the year 1649. This quintessence would have come from the spleens of plague victims. Now, they didn't end up carrying out this plan, but the mention is, in fact, the first written record of biological warfare."

Adrian stilled at her father's mention of plague victims, dread rising in her chest. "What if that's it?" she asked slowly. "The weapon. What if it's a bioweapon—a modern day plague?"

Robert and Nick both looked equally disturbed, as Adrian continued, "It could be the reason why they're so focused on this letter that mentions a doctor creating a poison."

"But the Black Death wasn't until almost two centuries after this letter," Nick said.

"There were other waves of plague that swept over Europe before and after the Black Death," Adrian countered. "Remember Archaia Sofia's mantra? It was all about destruction. This branch is also seeking destruction—and what better way to do that than a modern day plague?"

"Jesus," Nick muttered, closing his eyes.

The more Adrian thought about it, the more it made a sort of dark sense. Unleashing an ancient weapon on the modern world, just like Stephanos wanted to do with Greek fire.

"That sounds feasible," Robert said grimly. "Venice was hit hard by the plague, and given the

Dieci's focus on both Venice, Dubrovnik, and this letter..."

"A doctor in Istanbul around the twelfth century," Adrian said, retraining her focus on the letter, trying not to panic at the thought of a modern day plague. They would stop the Dieci before it came to that . . . they had to. "What links Istanbul to Venice?"

"First, we need to go back in time to when Istanbul was known as Constantinople," Robert said.

"It became Rome's new imperial capital in the east, while Rome remained the western capital. In fact, it was initially named New Rome until Emperor Constantine did the very common practice of naming the capital after himself. Constantinople remained a city of prime importance, not just as part of the eastern Roman Empire—or the Byzantine Empire, which it came to be known, but also the later short-lived Latin and longer-lived Ottoman empires. But the twelfth century is when Venice and Constantinople become inextricably entwined."

"Constantinople was incredibly wealthy and an important stop on the Silk Road. Where wealth is, trade follows. At this time, the Venetians were favored by the Byzantine emperor," Robert continued, "which resulted in a monopoly by them. This angered merchants from other Italian city-states as well as native merchants in the area. Tensions rose to the point that, after a group of Venetians attacked the Genoese in their quarter in Constantinople, Venetians were arrested on mass—not just in Constantinople—but all throughout the Byzantine Empire. A sort of cold war followed with Venetians attacking the empire indirectly by allying with its enemies, until finally there was a restoration of relations ten years later or so in the 1180s."

"The mass arrests—that explains the revenge the letter refers to," Adrian said. "But what about this doctor that—"

A sudden screeching alarm interrupted them. Robert hurried over to the monitor by the door that provided the security feed, and Adrian froze in panic.

A car was approaching the house.

CHAPTER 17

Čibača, Croatia
7:02 AM

Adrian, Nick and Robert raced out the back door. Robert took the lead, hurrying along the path of the bluff overlooking the beach, moving quickly away from the house.

Behind them, Adrian heard a car screeching up to the front of the house, and panic speared her chest. They increased their pace; Adrian could see where her father was leading them—toward a set of stairs that led down to the beach below.

"This way," Robert hissed. He turned and made his way down the stairs, with Adrian and Nick following suit. They had to move carefully, as the old stone steps were craggy and unsteady. Her father stumbled, and Nick reached forward to steady him as they continued to make their way down.

Once they reached the beach, they stayed tucked into the shadows of the bluff as they raced down it at a jog, the only sound their quick breaths and the pounding of the surf on the shore. Adrian strained her ears but didn't hear any sign of pursuers. Still, they continued at a jog for what seemed like a half an hour until they reached another set of stairs carved into the bluff.

This set of stairs led to a narrow dirt road that curved away from the bluff. They followed it at a quick pace until it made an abrupt turn to the left, leading into a small patch of forest.

Robert stopped walking, grinning at something in the patch of trees. Adrian followed his gaze, surprise filling her. An old Volkswagen was parked there.

"Hello, gorgeous," Robert said, approaching the car. He squatted down and ran his hands along the car's undercarriage, straightening with a set of keys.

"It always helps to have a backup plan. This getaway car was my idea—Ollie didn't think it was necessary, but I'm glad he listened to me," Robert said, moments later, as they sped down a dirt road that led out of the forest. "I don't know how they found us. If they've gotten to Ollie . . ." His voice trailed off, his expression shadowing with grief.

Adrian reached out to touch his arm in a gesture of comfort. Robert expelled a breath, as if forcing himself to focus.

"My only other friend and contact besides Ollie

and Ivan is Erasmo. He just happens to live where we need to go next. Istanbul."

Istanbul, Turkey
9:06 AM

VITTORIA GAZED out the window of her private plane as it landed, taking in the city of Istanbul in the far distance, dark memories assailing her.

Istanbul had been one of her and her late husband's favorite cities; they had even honeymooned here. Ever since she'd looked at the photo of her husband and son back in Venice, more and more memories of her life before had come flooding back.

Vittoria had gotten her dual degree in medicine and biology at Oxford, where she'd met her husband, Ben. They had both been idealists, wanting to make the world a better place with the emerging field of synthetic biology. Vittoria had distanced herself from her mother and the Dieci, not wanting anything to do with the organization and its dark goals. She'd foolishly thought there were better, less destructive ways to bring about change. She'd believed that whole-heartedly, until that terrible day when Ben and her son Massimo were killed.

It had been a bright and sunny morning when Ben told her he was taking their son to the playground at Gülhane Park, a large public park next to the Topkapi Palace, while Vittoria attended a conference. She had kissed her husband lingeringly on the lips before embracing her son, who was eager to get out of her arms to get to the park. She'd watched with a smile as they left the apartment they were renting for their few weeks stay in the city. If she had known that was the last time she'd ever see them again, alive, she would have held on to both of them, refusing to let them out of her sight.

Two hours later, just a couple of blocks from where her son cheerfully scooted down a slide and swung on the swings while her husband photographed him and took videos, a suicide bomber detonated his vest, killing her husband and son, along with hundreds of others, instantly.

Vittoria's grief had been a black hole from which she thought she would never emerge. Her mother, whom she had been estranged from, reentered her life. Valentina told Vittoria that what happened to her family proved that the world was beyond redemption, that she could still bring about change.

"The ancient wisdom teaches us that destruction is the only way to renewal. It is the only path to a world where innocents like your husband and son will never come to harm," Valentina had murmured, gazing into Vittoria's tear-filed eyes.

It didn't take long for Vittoria's grief to turn to anger, then determination. Her mother was right.

The world as it was . . . it was beyond redemption. Fundamentally broken. A cleansing was needed, a renewal.

She'd officially joined the Dieci, and after her mother's death she'd taken her place as one of its leaders, determined to see their plans through to the end. She used her medical knowledge to help advance their goal . . . the ultimate bioweapon.

From the very beginning, humanity's weakness ultimately came from the very small—pathogens. It was the most effective weapon that would bring humanity to its knees. Her lab in Geneva was working on creating the ultimate pathogen, stemming from the bacterium, Yersinia pestis, which had caused the Black Death. But she would pair it with a carefully engineered virus, making it hundreds of times more deadly. The Dieci alone would have the vaccine, which her lab was developing along with the virus. The pathogen was the only way to give the world the restart it needed, a cleansing to start anew.

Yet none of the samples they'd tested were potent enough, and that was why the key was so important. The archives of the Dieci told of the key, hidden for centuries since the days of the original cleansing, the Black Death. It was a particularly lethal strain that would bring about the end . . . the renewal the world so desperately needed.

CHAPTER 18

Terate, Italy
9:15 AM

Cora studied the kindling in the wood stove, waiting for it to catch fire. This was her third attempt, and her frustration, along with the anxiety that filled her ever since she'd been forced from her home, was increasing.

She looked around the rustic kitchen. She and Ivan were in an old farmhouse in a village a couple of hours away from Milan. Ivan informed her they would stay here for the time being, not giving her any information beyond that. When she'd asked who the farmhouse belonged to he'd just told her brusquely, "A trusted friend."

She'd decided to keep herself busy by attempting to use the archaic-looking wood stove in the kitchen to make some tea; Ivan had provided the wood and firelighters before heading into the village to get more groceries.

"You are doing it wrong."

She turned to find Ivan hovering in the doorway, a characteristic scowl on his face. He set down the bag of groceries and approached. He knelt down by the door to the stove, moving it further ajar and using another firelighter to set the kindling ablaze. After a few moments, the kindling flared to life.

"I left groceries in the next room," he said gruffly, straightening and heading out of the kitchen.

Cora watched him go, suddenly desperate for company, to not be alone with her worried thoughts, which had been racing throughout the long flight and the journey from the airport to the farmhouse. Ivan had barely spoken to her throughout the entire journey.

"How did you come to be friends with my husband?" she blurted.

Ivan paused, glancing back at her. "He is a good man," he said simply. Again, he started to leave, but Cora stopped him.

"Ivan . . . look, I don't know how long we're going to be here. We might as well get to know each other. I grew up in Maryland, met and fell in love with my husband in college, and I have the most amazing daughter. An exciting night for me is a glass of wine and a romantic comedy, which my daughter hates, but she indulges me and watches them with me. I think together we've watched hundreds since Robert went missing. I've always been good at numbers, so I became an accountant. I don't know how I got looped into all of this . . . this is my daughter's arena. I honestly don't know where Adrian gets her bravery from. Certainly not me. Just a spider is enough to scare me beyond measure."

Cora knew she was rambling, but it felt good to talk, to get out of her own head. To her surprise, Ivan seemed to listen intently to every word of said rambling. She even thought his lips twitched with amusement when she mentioned her love of romantic comedies.

"I promised your husband I will keep you safe until you can be reunited," he said finally. "That is all."

"But why would you go to such lengths to help him?" Cora pressed, both genuinely curious and slightly embarrassed by her word salad. Ivan's expression shuttered, and he looked away from her.

"I have a son," he said shortly. "He—"

He stopped abruptly, shaking his head as if to prevent himself from sharing any more information. Ivan turned, stomping out of the kitchen. Cora watched him go, a realization dawning. She trailed him to the next room, where he was unloading the groceries onto the table.

"They're doing the same thing to you, aren't they?" she pressed. "Forcing you to work for them in exchange for your son's life?"

He stiffened, and she could see he was trying to keep his expression neutral, but a deep pain flared in his eyes.

A sudden, burning hatred for the Dieci, for what they'd done to Robert and their family, to Ivan, and to countless others, flared to life in her chest. She wasn't like her fierce, brave, globe-trotting daughter or her husband who had gone through God knows what. She was just an aging accountant who lived in suburban Virginia. But she suddenly felt the need to *do* something.

I'm just an accountant. Cora stilled. It was something she'd always been uncommonly good at . . . numbers. Money was just numbers. Everyone operated using money, even the bad guys. *Especially* the bad guys. Given the sophistication of the Dieci, it had to have some sort of money network . . . which meant they could be tracked.

"You want to take these guys down as badly as my husband does, don't you?" she asked slowly.

Ivan just gave her a gruff nod. He'd stopped unpacking the groceries and was studying her, seeming to realize she'd come to a revelation.

"Then I have an idea," she said. "But I need you to tell me every detail you know about the Dieci."

~

Istanbul, Turkey
11:27 AM

THE LARGEST CITY IN TURKEY, its population teeming with over fifteen million souls, Istanbul was an economic and cultural hub, an ancient crossroads between Europe and Asia that straddled the Bosporous Strait.

Its dramatic architecture spoke of its past rule by the Byzantines and the Ottomans, from the ancient Walls of Constantinople, the Sultan Ahmed Mosque, known as the Blue Mosque, to the Topkapi Palace. It was a city both steeped in history and modernity, with contemporary buildings and skyscrapers that neighbored its more ancient structures.

They had flown from Dubrovnik to Istanbul International Airport using fake passports provided by her father's contact, Erasmo. Robert drove them through the bustling streets of the city in their rental car, and Adrian took in the sights, from the magnificent Hagia Sophia to the lively Taksim Square as they drove toward Fener district, where Erasmo lived.

Prior to her father's disappearance, she had loved Istanbul, appreciating its storied history. But now dark memories filled her as she recalled traveling to Istanbul after her father's disappearance, only to hit brick wall after brick wall with the local authorities. She could clearly remember making her way back to her hotel, breaking down into sobs as she realized her father may be gone forever.

She met her father's gaze, and his expression

was pained. He also had dark memories from this city as well.

They soon entered the Fener district, which had once been home to the Jewish and Greek populations of the city. Now it was a quieter neighborhood than the more touristic parts of the city, where many locals lived. Lying along the banks of the Golden Horn, an inlet of the Bosphorus Strait, it was dotted with cafes, bistros, colorful traditional Ottoman houses, and charming cobblestoned streets.

Robert parked on a side street, and they trailed him to one of the Ottoman houses, this one painted a shade of dark blue. Just as Robert raised his hand to knock, the door opened, and a hand yanked him inside, a gun pressed to the base of his throat by a stout yet muscular Turkish man.

CHAPTER 19

Panicked, Adrian and Nick scrambled forward, but Robert held up his hands, keeping his gaze trained on the man.

The man had shoulder-length, dark hair peppered with gray, and silver eyes that pierced her father with a suspicious glare.

"*Fac fortia et patere,*" Robert said.

Adrian recognized the Latin motto, it meant to do brave deeds and endure. The phrase seemed to be some sort of secret code between them, as the man gazed at Robert for several tense moments before lowering the gun. His hard expression dissipated, and he offered her father an apologetic smile.

"Sorry about that, my friend," he said. His English was strong, with only the slightest hint of a Turkish accent. "But I can't be too careful."

He turned to them with a warm smile, as if he hadn't just pressed a gun to her father's throat. "I'm

Erasmo. And you must be Adrian, Robert's little girl," he said. "Thankfully, she doesn't look like you, Robert."

Adrian glared at Erasmo, anger still coursing through her. Her father stepped forward, placing a placating hand on her arm.

"It's OK. We have a . . . system between us. We never know who's been compromised. And after what happened to Ollie . . . "

Erasmo's joviality faded, and he looked at Robert with concern. "What happened to Oliver?"

Robert gave him a grim look. "There's much I need to catch you up on."

THEY SAT around a table on Erasmo's balcony that overlooked the colorful homes of the district. From her vantage point Adrian could glimpse the glittering waters of the Golden Horn. Erasmo had served them what he called a typical Turkish breakfast, complete with cups of black tea and an assortment of cured meats, bread, fruit and cheeses.

"I am ashamed to say I was once a member of the Dieci," Erasmo said, his gray eyes shadowing. "Membership tends to pass down from father to son, mother to daughter. My father was a member. I naively thought it was mainly a historical society. Before I worked in Turkish intelligence, I studied history, specifically the history of my country, and Istanbul. In another life, I would have been a boring history professor. It's why I left Turkish intelligence, actually. I wanted to go into academia. But then I found out the true goals of the Dieci . . ." He trailed off, pain flickering across his face.

Her father reached out to give Erasmo's shoulder a comforting squeeze, subtly shaking his head. Adrian suspected there was more to Erasmo's story.

Erasmo gave Robert a look of regret. "Again, I am sorry for threatening you, my friend. But—"

"You're forgiven," Robert said firmly. He turned to give Adrian and Nick a long look, as if daring them to challenge him. It reminded her of the looks he'd given her when she was a disobedient child.

Adrian just gave her father a gruff nod. She was still annoyed with Erasmo for threatening her father, but there was no time to hold grudges. They were here on a mission.

Robert filled Erasmo in on everything that had happened since they'd all met up in Dubrovnik, including the coded letter and their theory of the Dieci seeking to create a bioweapon, ending with the ambush at Oliver's home. Erasmo fell silent, his brow furrowed with worry.

"I'll have my contacts check on Oliver," Erasmo said, though he didn't look optimistic. "As for your theory of a bioweapon . . . I fear you may be right. The higher-ups are keeping it under wraps, but there are rumors of a lab where they're running tests on potential pathogens."

Adrian stilled, a chill going through her. "They're looking for some sort of key—something from the past to help them with this bioweapon," she said. "Do you have any idea what it could be?"

Erasmo considered her question for a moment, drumming his fingers on the table. "I know the Venetians dabbled in bioweaponry against their enemies in medieval times, during the height of their power. That could be why the letter they stole was so important—the one that mentions a doctor in Istanbul. Maybe that doctor figured something out, something they could still use today. There's no way to know for certain until we find out exactly who this doctor was. And that itself is a problem. A doctor in Istanbul from this time period covers a wide pool. Was it a local doctor from Istanbul? A Venetian doctor who happened to be in Istanbul? Or a Byzantine court doctor?"

"Whoever this doctor was, he was helping the Venetians," Robert said. "The letter made that clear."

"This is going to be a bit of a needle in a historical haystack," Erasmo said, "but we can dig into records from the Byzantine period to see if there's any mention of notable local doctors from this time period. Records from that era are tricky to come by here in Istanbul—most were lost during and after the Ottoman conquest, and many surviving documents are kept in monasteries outside of the country. But there are a couple of places we can check here—the archives at the Tekfur Palace Museum and the library of Istanbul University."

"We need to move fast," Robert said. "The Dieci has had the letter for at least a few weeks, which means they've decrypted it by now. They're way ahead of us."

"*If* they've found anything at all," Erasmo returned. "And you know how much I like a challenge," he added with a wink.

He got to his feet, the determination on his face chasing away the playfulness. "Now. Let's go stop these bastards from finding this key they're looking for."

CHAPTER 20

Istanbul, Turkey
1:48 PM

Tekfur Palace, or the Palace of Porphyrogenitus, was one of the few surviving Byzantine palaces in Istanbul, dating to back to the thirteenth century. The Greek name of the palace, Porphyrogenitus, meant 'born to the purple', referring to the birthplace of the emperor's heir, while the Turkish name, Tekfur, meant 'Palace of the Sovereign'. It was an imperial residence in the waning days of the Byzantine empire, and after the fall of Constantinople it served as everything from a brothel, a menagerie, to a pottery workshop.

It was abandoned by the early twentieth century, and underwent restorations in the twenty-first century before its current transformation into a museum. With its restored Byzantine facade and interior of marble columns, along with an arcade that looked out onto the expansive courtyard, it was hard not to admire the palace and the extensive restoration work it had undergone.

Adrian had to force herself to focus and not admire all the architecture; she and her father had an important task. They had decided to divide and conquer, with Adrian and her father going to Tekfur Palace, while Erasmo and Nick had gone to the main library of Istanbul University. Adrian had suggested the teams, surprised at the ferocity of how much she didn't want to let her father out of her sight . . . as if he would disappear again. She wondered if the feeling would ever go away.

Once they reached the records room, she and her father gave the archivist their cover story, that Robert was a professor and she was his teaching assistant researching the relations between Venetian and Byzantine leadership in the twelfth and thirteenth centuries. They were hoping this information would give them more context while searching for this mysterious doctor.

"You might want to start by looking into Enrico Dandolo," the archivist, a young woman who introduced herself as Damia, told them. "He was a doge of Venice who was furious with Constantinople over the mass arrests of Venetians. He became doge years after the arrests but they still angered him; it's well-documented."

Adrian and her father took Damia's advice, combing through the documents that she'd provided for them. Reviewing the records, Adrian learned that Enrico Dandolo was born into a powerful Venetian family and was elected as the doge of Venice late in life, when he was eighty-four. In the twelfth century, before he was elected doge, he visited Constantinople to negotiate reparations for Venetians after the mass arrests with Emperor Andronikos, and the Venetians were released.

Adrian and Robert searched through each document that Damia provided them, hoping to find any reference to a prominent doctor associated with Dandolo. They learned that his wife, Contessa, handled his affairs while he traveled, along with his brother and a family friend named Fillippo. But there was no mention of a doctor.

Frustration coiled in Adrian's belly, thinking of Erasmo's words. They were indeed searching for a needle in a historical haystack. She was on the verge of suggesting that they redirect their search focus when she stumbled upon something.

Adrian went still, reading and rereading the document.

"Adrian?" Her father was looking at her expectantly.

She slid the document she'd been reading toward him. "This is a copy of a letter sent by a foreign diplomat visiting the Byzantine court around the same time as the letter we found in Dubrovnik was written."

"OK," her father said slowly, skimming the letter.

"Here's what I found out before stumbling on that document—before Emperor Andronikos, a woman named Maria of Antioch ruled the empire as regent for her son. She wasn't popular with her subjects, as she was a Westerner by birth, and she pretty openly favored the Italian merchants. The *Venetian* merchants."

Robert straightened at this, his eyes going wide. Adrian smiled and continued, "It was this unrest around her rule that enabled Andronikos to seize power. Andronikos had her imprisoned, killed and later, her son killed as well, before seizing power for himself." She pointed to the document she'd slid toward him. "This letter mentions a private doctor Maria had up to the time of her murder, rumored to be her lover—though she was so disliked by contemporaries rumors like these are probably false. This letter even hints that she may not have been murdered after all, but fled with her personal doctor."

Robert nodded slowly, the realization dawning. "So this doctor mentioned could have feasibly been working with the empress—who favored the Venetians—on some type of bioweapon that could destroy their enemies. A weapon the Dieci is now looking for."

"Exactly. Dad, this could be it. We need to find her trail before they do," Adrian said, her voice rising with urgency.

Robert studied her for a long moment, a sudden indecipherable emotion flaring in his eyes.

"What?"

"It's just—that's the first time I've heard you call me 'Dad' in over a decade. There was a time when I never thought I'd hear your voice again, much less . . . "

Without thinking, Adrian reached out to cover her father's hand with her own. Robert offered her a smile that she returned, and they shared a moment of shared emotion, until Adrian withdrew her hand. "I should loop in Nick and Erasmo."

As she dialed Nick's number, her father let out a sharp intake of breath.

Adrian looked up, startled, as a lovely, dark-haired woman entered, trailed by a tall and imposing female guard.

"Adrian West," the woman said smoothly, with only a hint of an Italian accent, her cold dark eyes trained on Adrian. "It's so nice to finally meet you in person."

CHAPTER 21

Istanbul, Turkey
2:19 PM

Nick was starting to think he got the raw end of the deal by being paired with Erasmo.

He knew the reason the pairings had ended up this way; Adrian was determined not to let her father out of her sight and given the circumstances, he could hardly blame her.

Erasmo was . . . odd. He had come across all types of characters during his time with the bureau, but Erasmo was one of the more distinctive. While he had seemed somewhat normal at breakfast, his oddities had become more apparent during their time alone together. Erasmo had an eerie habit of not breaking eye contact, telling rambling, cryptic stories that went nowhere, and, most irritatingly, asking inappropriate personal questions. During the drive to the university library, Erasmo had calmly asked about his and Adrian's lovemaking frequency. Nick had remained tight-lipped, his annoyance rising, relieved when they finally reached Istanbul University.

Founded in the fifteenth century after the Ottomans had conquered Constantinople, it was now one of the most prestigious universities in the world, boasting distinguished alumni that included prime ministers and Nobel Laureates. The main campus was rich with history, centered on Beyazit Square, a construction of Constantine the Great, with ancient ruins from both the Roman and Byzantine eras dotting the grounds. Despite the historical origins of the campus, the main library was in a distinctly modern building across the street from a bustling tram line.

The staff seemed to know Erasmo and greeted him warmly, directing them toward a section of the library dedicated to records from the city's Byzantine era. Together, Nick and Erasmo proceeded to scour royal court records from the twelfth and thirteenth centuries . . . anything that could point them to this doctor. But they weren't finding anything significant.

Nick was just about to give up when he stumbled across documents detailing the history of Istanbul's Zeyrek Mosque, which had once been a Christian monastery. The part that jumped out to him was the fact that it had once housed an active hospital—in the same time period that they were searching for this doctor.

"What do you know about Zeyrek Mosque?" Nick asked Erasmo. As odd as he found the man, he was a fountain of knowledge about Istanbul's history.

"Ah, the underrated and barely visited Zeyrek Mosque, hovering in the shadow of the Hagia Sophia," Erasmo said, leaning back in his chair. "After the Hagia Sophia, it's the second largest Byzantine church still standing here in Istanbul. Like many Christian places of worship, it was converted from a monastery to a mosque after the Ottoman conquest of Constantinople and named after Molla Zeyrek, a scholar."

"The monastery once housed a hospital," Nick said, giving Erasmo a significant look. He pointed at one of the documents before sliding it across the table. "It says here that the monastery was the Venetian headquarters for clergy during the thirteenth century after the Fourth Crusade, and when the Latin Empire occupied Constantinople."

"I did not know that," Erasmo said, looking genuinely surprised that he didn't know something about Istanbul's history. "That could be very significant indeed."

"I'm going to reach out to Adrian and Robert—see what they've found so far," Nick said, but as soon as he took out his phone, it began to buzz with Adrian's caller ID. "Speak of the devil."

He answered. At first there was silence on the

other end, and it took him a few moments to understand what he was hearing.

Once he did, panic filled him and he met Erasmo's eyes, his face going pale.

∼

2:47 PM

"I HAVE men stationed throughout the museum who won't hesitate to start killing people. I'll start with your father," the woman continued. The female guard stepped forward, aiming her pistol at Robert.

Adrian forced herself to remain calm, keeping her gaze trained on the woman, glad that Damia had excused herself to go to another department several minutes before; she'd inadvertently gotten herself out of danger. But she didn't know how long Damia would stay away. She needed to think fast.

Adrian had quickly slipped her cell phone in her pocket after Nick had answered, praying that he could hear everything being said. She needed to buy time, but it was hard to stay calm when there was a pistol trained on her father for the second time in less than a few hours.

"Robert," the woman said, still looking at Adrian as she addressed him, "my mother would be so disappointed. You know the price of treachery."

"I do, Vittoria," Robert said calmly. Despite the

gun pointed at him, his entire focus was on the woman. "But I can help you. Just let my daughter go."

"You are not the one calling the shots here, Doctor West. I am," Vittoria returned, her eyes narrowing. "We know you've read the Dubrovnik letter. What else have you found?"

Adrian debated lying, but she didn't want to take any risks with her father's life, especially considering what they'd found was lying in plain view on the table. Vittoria raised a brow, giving her an expectant look.

"We found reference to a doctor working with Maria of Antioch, a Byzantine empress who was friendly toward the Venetians. It's all there," Adrian said in a rush, gesturing to the records on the table.

Vittoria started toward the table when the sound of sirens and screeching tires pulling into the parking lot assaulted their ears. Adrian's heart leapt with hope. *Nick*. Realizing that he and Erasmo couldn't get to them in time, he must have called the police, giving them the opportunity to escape.

Adrian sprang into action.

Bracing herself against the table, she leapt to her feet and lifted it, pushing it toward Vittoria and her guard. Both of them stumbled back, startled, as she and Robert whirled, racing toward the back exit.

They darted toward the shelves in the back of the room, using them as cover as they scrambled away. She could hear Vittoria and her guard's footsteps hurrying after them. Her heart was in her throat as she and her father reached the back exit, shoving open the door and darting out.

To her relief, a thick crowd of museum guests were evacuating; Adrian and Robert rushed forward, blending into the crowd. She heard the door to the records room slam open as Vittoria and her guard rushed out, but Adrian purposefully moved in front of a tall man and his wife, using them as cover as they made their way out.

Her pulse raced as she and her father kept pace with the crowd before ducking out of a side exit. They remained still, tensely waiting to see if Vittoria had picked up their trail, but no one approached them. For now, at least, they had lost them.

After several more tense moments, Adrian grabbed her father's arm, and they hurried away from the museum.

CHAPTER 22

*R*obert and Adrian raced through the winding streets that led away from the museum and into the Ayvansaray neighborhood, which was filled with historical monuments that traced the city's history from the Byzantine to Ottoman eras, from mosques that had once been churches to the remains of the walls of Constantinople that had defended the great city from foreign attacks.

Once they were out of the vicinity of the museum, they slowed to a brisk walk, keeping careful track of their surroundings. They eventually made their way through a series of residential streets until they reached a more commercial area, teeming with shops, hotels and cafes. After venturing deeper into the cornucopia of streets, Adrian spotted a small but crowded cafe. She gestured to her father to follow her, and they made their way inside.

Adrian surreptitiously looked around as Robert ordered two Turkish black teas for them. From the variety of languages ranging from English to Turkish, she could both hear and see that the cafe was filled with tourists and locals alike, none of whom seemed to be interested in her and her father, besides a couple of curious glances.

Once they had their teas, Adrian purposefully sat next to a large group of tourists near the back door, where they could make a quick exit if need be. Still keeping track of her surroundings, she sent Nick and Erasmo a text letting them know where they were.

"Who was that woman?" Adrian whispered, putting down her phone.

"I only know her first name. She's the daughter of the woman who took me captive, Valentina. She seems to have taken Valentina's place since her death. I've had little interaction with her, but from what I've heard, she's as vicious as her mother. Perhaps even more so."

"How'd she know we'd be there? Do you think she's been following us, or was it just happenstance?"

"We've been careful . . . they may have already been there and seen us enter. We are looking for the same thing, after all."

"And why did you offer to sacrifice yourself—again? She would have just killed you. You've already sacrificed yourself enough."

Her father stiffened, returning her reprimanding look with a hard glare of his own. "I will always sacrifice myself for you and your mother."

"I know what you're willing to do, believe me. Again, I can get you to safety. The bureau has resources—"

But Robert had held up his hand, shaking his head. "No. I'm going to see this through to the end."

Before Adrian could reply, two tall Turkish men entered the cafe, looking around. She stiffened, relaxing only when they joined another group of men who sat in the center of the cafe.

"We should keep moving. Nick and Erasmo can meet us out back," Adrian said.

Her father thankfully didn't protest, and they slipped out the back door that led to a narrow alleyway.

They hurried down the alley, freezing at the sound of a car barreling toward them.

Panic filling her veins, Adrian jerked her father back against the wall as the car screeched to a halt right in front of them. But relief washed over her as she recognized the car—and its driver.

Erasmo poked his head out, offering them a smile. "Need a ride?"

Vrânceanu Institute of Historical Archaeology

Bucharest, Romania
5:17 PM

Polina parked across the street from the institute, sinking down low in her seat. Only a day ago she would have felt ridiculous about what she was doing, but after she'd overheard what Mikhail and those men were discussing...

She expelled a breath, forcing down her rising panic. She'd requested vacation time, telling Mikhail that she was going to take an extended vacation to see her family. By the look on Mikhail's face, he'd bought her story and looked relieved, which only fueled her suspicion even more.

In reality, she'd left her apartment, checked into a small hotel under a different name, and rented a car. She had to confirm if what she'd heard was truly what she suspected. If it was...

Fear gripped her, and she tightened her hold on the steering wheel. *One step at a time, Polina.*

She knew Mikhail's hours like clockwork, and so she'd come to the institute to follow him to wherever he went after work, something she was going to do for the next three weeks of her 'vacation'. Polina waited for twenty minutes until she saw Mikhail's familiar form leave the building, watching as he entered his car and pulled away.

Polina started her car and followed him from a distance as he made his way from the institute and through the streets of central Bucharest.

Traffic was heavy, but that made it easier to tail

Mikhail through the bustling streets, making her way past the city's major sights, from the Palace of Parliament, the streets of Old Town, to the old Roman Athanaeum.

Usually, Polina would enjoy the sights of the city she had made her home. She had grown up in a small village not far from Bucharest, a village her family had called home for generations, yet she had fallen in love with Bucharest when she came to work at the institute, with its modern big city charm yet long history.

But now she could only focus on trailing Mikhail's dark grey Renault through the streets, trepidation coursing through her.

Mikhail took the Basarab Overpass bridge across the Dâmbovița River, which wound its way throughout the city, to the outskirts of Bucharest until he reached the residential neighborhood of Pipera. Polina frowned as she realized where they were . . . Mikhail's neighborhood. She'd come to his home for the holiday parties he'd held for his employees at least twice. Defeat settled over her as she realized Mikhail was just going home. Regret mixed with hope was starting to rise within her . . . maybe she was reading too much into what she'd heard.

Still, she followed him all the way to his home, spotting a familiar car parked outside, a blue Dacia Logan. She frowned. It was Florin's car.

Parking several homes away, she watched as Florin emerged from Mikhail's home just as he got out of his car, looking pale and shaken. Florin approached Mikhail, speaking rapidly and waving his hands in the air as Mikhail responded with what looked like annoyance; the two seemed to be in a heated argument.

Finally, Mikhail's front door swung open, and two imposing men stepped out. She stilled. They were the same two men Polina had seen Mikhail with at the institute.

Florin took them in, his body going stiff. The sight of them seemed to scare him, and he lowered his head, falling silent and turning to head back into the house. The two men nodded at Mikhail and followed suit.

Looking pleased, Mikhail cast a look around at the street. Alarmed, Polina sank down in her seat. After several moments, he headed inside.

She watched him disappear inside his home, recalling what she'd overheard back at the institute with crystal clarity.

"Extraction of the pathogen has proven difficult," Mikhail said. *"I don't know if it will be viable. The samples are highly degraded."*

"She'll want to look at whatever you've been able to extract," one of the men replied. *"And she'll expect a full report once you go to meet her in Genoa."*

Extraction of the pathogen. Those words had struck her like a bullet, and all the secrecy made sense.

Now, seeing Florin only confirmed her suspicions. She knew Mikhail had a sophisticated lab in the basement of his home.

Her boss, with Florin's help, was trying to extract a pathogen from ancient bones.

A pathogen that had killed millions.

CHAPTER 23

Istanbul, Turkey
5:57 PM

Adrian and the others entered the safe house in central Istanbul, a contemporary three-story home with several guest rooms, minimalist decor, and a rooftop with a panoramic view of the city. Nick let out a low whistle as they stepped inside, taking it in.

"Good job, Vince."

Adrian smiled, turning her focus to her father and Erasmo, who were warily regarding the interior of the house.

After filling in Erasmo and Nick on what had happened at the museum with Vittoria, she had convinced Robert and Erasmo that they needed to reach out to the task force to find a safe house. They couldn't risk going back to Erasmo's home in case Vittoria had tracked them there. Robert and Erasmo had only reluctantly agreed.

In order to use the safe house, Adrian and Nick came clean to Briggs about what they were doing in Istanbul. Erasmo had pulled his car onto an empty side street so that Nick and Adrian could step out and place a call Briggs.

They'd told Briggs everything about the Dieci and her father's captivity, the Dieci's plans, the confrontation with the shooter back in Dubrovnik, and their encounter with Vittoria.

"I can't say I'm thrilled about this. You two going rogue isn't exactly surprising," Briggs had said, heaving a sigh. "But I knew you both were up to something when you had Vince run a photo through facial recognition. I was suspicious of you both actually being capable of taking a vacation."

"Hey," Nick replied in a tone of mock offense. "We will take an actual vacation—one day. And tell Vince he's a traitor."

"Adrian, I am glad to hear your father is alive," Briggs continued, his tone softening. "I'll keep that fact under wraps until this is all over."

"Thank you," Adrian said, both surprised and relieved. Her father's disappearance was well known at the bureau, which had investigated it before Adrian became an agent.

"I'll reach out to the local authorities in Dubrovnik to deal with the shooter—and they may have information about his identity. I'll have the task force look into this Vittoria person and into

Lucija Novak's disappearance as well," Briggs added. "Keep me posted. I'm asking nicely, but it's really an order."

"Touché," Nick replied before ending the call. Shortly after that, Vince had gotten back to them with the address of the safe house in central Istanbul, a place typically used by the CIA.

Now, they headed further inside the safe house. "I'm going to check for listening devices," Erasmo said, clearly still suspicious.

Adrian, Nick and Robert made their way to the spacious kitchen, finding MRE packs, which were pre-packaged meals typically reserved for military use, stored in the pantry. They were beef stew, and Nick heated them up on the stove as Adrian and Robert sat down at the table. Erasmo entered, joining them.

"I assume you found nothing?" Nick asked, raising an eyebrow. Erasmo just grunted in response, and Nick grinned. "See? Sometimes we Americans can be trustworthy."

"Sometimes," Erasmo replied, but his lips twitched with amusement.

"The woman we encountered at the museum—Vittoria. Do you know anything about her?" Adrian asked Erasmo.

"Like your father, I know very little about her. She keeps a low profile, even amongst the leadership," Erasmo replied. "But if she's here, that means the Dieci also believe the answers are here in Istanbul."

"Adrian picked up a promising lead with the empress Maria of Antioch and her doctor," Robert said, giving her a proud look. "But we don't know how to pick up their trail."

"We may have found something as well," Nick said, glancing briefly at Erasmo.

As he told them about Zeyrek Mosque, Adrian felt a ripple of hope . . . this was a promising lead. As they ate, they continued to discuss the mosque and what they could find there, as well as theories as to where Maria and this doctor could have gone, until she noticed it was pitch black outside and everyone looked weighed down by fatigue, especially her father.

As Robert and Erasmo retired to their respective guest rooms, Nick and Adrian headed up to the roof to take a breather before heading to bed.

Adrian looked out over the city, at the dark waters of the Bosphorus in the distance, the turrets of the Hagia Sophia arching into the sky, the domed older buildings adjacent to the modern buildings that illuminated the city with light. Nick wrapped his arms around her from behind, pressing his lips to the side of her neck. Adrian closed her eyes, leaning back into his arms.

"You had me worried, West," Nick murmured. "Calling the cops was an act of desperation. I wanted nothing more than to get to you."

"I know," Adrian returned, knowing she would have felt the same. "What you did was more than enough. It gave us the opportunity to get the hell out of there."

They fell silent, taking in the panoramic view that lay before them. Her thoughts returned to the empress and the doctor, wondering what they could be missing and what they'd gleaned from their leads that could push them further along.

"If Maria didn't die like the records tell us, and she and her doctor managed to flee Constantinople, we have no idea how to pick up their trail," she said, slipping out of Nick's arms and turning to face him.

"I think we've made too many assumptions," she said. "What if this doctor—a court doctor— worked for Emperor Andronikos, but remained loyal to the Venetians and Maria? Court doctors had to officially work for whomever was in power. We just assumed he ran off with Maria or left court. I bet it won't take much digging to see if we can find reference to him working for Andronikos."

Moments later, they were combing through the copies of records that Nick and Erasmo had brought back with them from the library, searching specifically through court appointments.

"Ding ding ding," Nick said with a grin, holding up a document. "I think we may have found our needle in the historical haystack."

Adrian studied it, hope filling her chest. The document was a court administrative record referencing Andronikos bringing in a new court doctor, as the previous one had left to go work at the hospital of the local monastery.

The same monastery Nick had told them about—the monastery that was now a mosque. Zeyrek Mosque

"That's not all. Look at that additional notation at the bottom," Nick added, "about where the previous doctor was trained."

Adrian followed his gaze, her body going still as she read the translated notation.

> Doctor not trained in Constantinople. Trained under the tutelage of the Venetians.

It was the connection to Venice that they were looking for.

CHAPTER 24

Terate, Italy
8:17 AM

Cora sat in front of Ivan's laptop at the small kitchen table, combing through what felt like the millionth financial database that she had access to thanks to her job at the accounting firm.

Ivan had told her everything he knew about how the Dieci functioned in terms of money transfers, and she was using that information to see if she could track down a financial trail. But they hid their tracks well, and she wasn't finding anything.

She leaned back in her chair, tears pricking at her eyes. Hours of stress and worry had taken their toll. Ivan had just left to head into town to replenish their supplies. He hadn't heard from Robert at all, so Cora was left wondering if her daughter and husband were safe, or even alive. She pushed back against that terrifying thought, getting to her feet and moving over to the coffeemaker to make herself a cup, needing to give her mind a break.

Looking out at the countryside through the kitchen window, she thought about how in different circumstances this might be a pleasant vacation. She and Robert had gone to Europe together only once, before Adrian was born, despite his status as a poor graduate student and Cora still being early in her career. They'd saved their pennies and taken a month to explore England, France and Italy.

They'd enjoyed their travels so much that they'd promised each other to retire together somewhere in Europe during their golden years. She'd thought about that promise many times in the years after Robert went missing, with the persistent—and ridiculous—thought that her husband couldn't be dead because they were going to retire in Europe together.

Cora wiped away her tears as she poured her coffee into a mug before making her way to the back door. She needed air and intended to walk the trail through the woods that Ivan had shown her. Like a concerned parent, he'd made her promise not to walk far and to maintain awareness of her surroundings. She understood his concern, but after just a couple of days of being here, she felt as safe as one could under these circumstances. The farmhouse was isolated, and she hadn't seen another soul other than Ivan. She just wished she knew for certain if Robert and Adrian were safe.

By the time she'd walked a bit down the trail, taking in the fresh air of the day, she felt calmer, and once again determined to keep looking into this organization. While her husband and daughter were out saving the world, she could do her part to help.

Cora returned to the farmhouse, stunned to see Ivan standing by the backdoor, his eyes wild with panic. At the sight of her, he stalked forward, roughly grabbing her arm and dragging her back inside, where he finally released her.

"Where did you go?" he snarled, his accent thicker than usual, looking so furious that Cora took a step back in fear.

"I—I went for a walk down the trail you showed me," she said shakily. "What—what's going on? Did something happen?"

Some unknown emotion flickered across Ivan's expression, and he looked away, shaking his head.

"No. Nothing new, but it is not safe. Until we get word of where to go next, you are to stay in the house."

His tone was harsh, and his words didn't seem like a suggestion—they seemed like an order. He glared at her until she nodded, and she watched as he turned to lock the door.

Cora studied him, her heart racing. She'd felt safe with him here, and it seemed as if they'd crossed some sort of invisible boundary ever since he'd told her about his son. But now . . . something had shifted.

For the first time since she'd met him, a frisson of fear wormed its way down her spine.

~

Istanbul, Turkey
9:03 AM

ERASMO PARKED a couple of kilometers away from Zeyrek Mosque. Adrian, Nick and her father each used the binoculars they'd found in the safe house to study it.

One of the few remaining buildings with Byzantine architecture in Istanbul, with its domed, vaulted ceilings and exterior made up of recessed bricks, it consisted of two former Eastern Orthodox churches and a chapel. The grounds of the mosque included a cafe and bookstore, along with a museum. From a quick online search, they'd learned that the museum had an archives room, detailing finds from the mosque's history. It was where they intended to search next.

After the revelation Nick and Adrian had discovered the night before, she and Nick had filled in Robert and Erasmo. They had readily agreed to come to the mosque, but decided to survey it from some distance away first to see if there were any obvious signs of Vittoria and her men there.

"Three o'clock," Nick said, lowering his binoculars. Adrian followed his gaze with her own binoculars, and dread pooled in her belly.

Directly across from the museum, a man wearing a dark suit sat in a black sedan, surveilling it.

"What are the odds of a well-dressed man staking out a museum?" Nick asked warily.

"I say we tackle this with teamwork," Erasmo said, turning to face them. "Nick and I can distract him while Adrian and Robert heads in through the back to get to the records room. We can all meet back at the safe house in two hours."

"Distract him?" Nick asked warily. "How?"

"You'll see, my friend," Erasmo said, giving him a conspiratorial wink.

Adrian could sense Nick's trepidation, but they needed to see what was here, especially if it could give them more information on this doctor. Nick heaved a sigh and offered a grudging nod.

Moments later, Adrian and Robert tucked themselves into the alcove of a nearby building, watching as Erasmo drove off with Nick.

Erasmo drove boldly toward the man's car, ramming into him from behind. The driver immediately straightened, glaring.

Erasmo grinned as the driver took in him and Nick. The driver stilled, looking as if he recognized Erasmo, Nick, or both of them—which Erasmo seemed to count on. Erasmo offered the man his middle finger before speeding away.

The driver took the bait, his car's tires screeching as he took off after Erasmo.

"That's one way to do it," her father said wryly, as he and Adrian hurried toward the mosque.

CHAPTER 25

11:17 AM
Istanbul, Turkey

Nick was pretty sure he was going to die.

He held on for dear life as Erasmo took side splitting turns down narrow streets, the driver hot on their heels—and the bastard was *grinning*. It felt as if they'd been speeding through the streets of Istanbul for hours, while Nick knew it was only minutes.

For all of Erasmo's reckless driving, he managed to evade the man chasing them, and soon pulled onto a narrow side street before taking an abrupt left, nearly plowing into a fruit vendor who let out a string of curses. Erasmo pulled up to the front of the safe house, turning to Nick.

"Grab your lovely girlfriend and her father," Erasmo said, scanning his rearview mirror. "I may have lost him for now, but I don't want to risk him picking up our trail."

Nick obliged, hurrying inside the safe house. To his relief, Adrian and Robert were both there, looking at him with alarm at his hasty entrance.

"We have to go—now."

∼

Thirty Minutes Ago

ADRIAN PACED the length of the living room of the safe house, gritting her teeth with frustration.

Their attempt to seek information at the mosque turned out to be a bust. As soon as they'd slipped inside using the rear entrance and made their way to the archives room, they spotted yet another imposing man hovering by the door, and the young archivist inside looked terrified. It didn't take much to discern that he was likely from the Dieci, like the driver.

Adrian and her father had snuck back out of the mosque and taken a cab to the safe house, frequently looking over their shoulder during the drive back. She'd hoped that Nick and Erasmo would have already returned, but the house was empty, and she was trying not to worry, reassuring herself that both men were highly capable of evading Vittoria's men.

On top of this disappointment, she had received a text from Athena Karras during the drive back to the safe house, informing her that she'd been unable to get any more information about the Dieci from members of the Greek branch of Archaia Sofia. She'd promised to let Adrian know if there were any developments, but Adrian doubted there would be any.

Now that they couldn't access the archives at the museum, they needed another way to find more information. Adrian thought about everything they'd learned so far.

The letter in Dubrovnik. The mysterious doctor helping the Venetians. The Dieci looking for a historical link to help them start a modern day plague.

They needed to find exactly what the Dieci was searching for in the present. In order to do that, they needed to start at the beginning.

"What do you know about the origins of the Black Death?" Adrian asked her father, turning to face him. "Where did it start?"

"The most accepted theory is that while it likely started in the east, the starting point for Europe was in Kaffa . . . now Feodosia, on the Crimean peninsula. It was a Genoese colony and trading port. In 1347, an army of Mongols laying siege to the city became ill, and hurled bodies of the dead over the city walls to infect its inhabitants. Infected Genoans fleeing the sickness returned to Italy, stopping along at various ports and inadvertently spreading the disease."

"I don't think it's a coincidence that Genoans,

ancient enemies of the Venetians, were the ones who transported the plague into Europe from Kaffa," Adrian said slowly.

"But how would that have worked?" Robert asked her with a puzzled frown. "Were the Venetians working with the Mongol army? The army picked up the plague from a source in the east."

"I don't know," Adrian said, "but I think there may be some connection. Is there something from the modern day that we can look into? Something that links to the origins of the plague?"

"That would probably be mass graves found in modern times," Robert said after a brief pause, moving over to the table and opening Erasmo's laptop. "To this day, archaeologists are still uncovering mass graves of plague victims."

"What about any finds near modern day Kaffa?" Adrian asked. "Anything recent?"

She moved to stand behind her father as he ran a search through an archaeological database that he had access to. After several moments, he paused, studying the screen.

"This could be something," he said. "Here's an article referencing the find of a mass grave not far from modern day Kaffa—Feodosia—around the time of the siege. The Vrânceanu Institute of Historical Archaeology is handling analysis of the remains. There's a name here—Doctor Polina Lysenko. She's one of the paleopathologists studying the bone samples."

The front door to the safe house crashed open.

Adrian shoved her father behind her, readying her weapon. But to her relief, it was Nick. He was pale and out of breath.

"We have to go—now."

Once they were all in the car with Erasmo, Nick turned to face Adrian and Robert. "We need to get out of this city—the Dieci's people are all over it."

Adrian thought about the recent find of the mass grave of plague victims in Feodosia, a place that was one of the Black Plague's origins. She had no doubt it was something the Dieci would have looked into, given their goal.

She recalled the paleopathologist her father had mentioned, Doctor Polina Lysenko. "There's someone who may be able to help us—in Bucharest."

CHAPTER 26

Istanbul, Turkey
12:11 PM

Vittoria ignored yet another incoming text from Paolo Marini. She knew he was seeking updates on what she'd found here in Istanbul.

If he and the other leaders knew of her most recent failure to capture West, they would again compare her to Stephanos, or unfavorably to her mother's superior leadership. Vittoria wondered briefly if they were right . . . if she should just lead the research team at the lab in Geneva, focusing on using her medical training to help achieve their goal.

But she immediately squashed the thought, Ben and Massimo's faces flashing in her mind. She wanted—needed—to be the one to bring the plan to fruition.

Vittoria closed her eyes and rubbed her temples, her frustration surging. She had posted her men at places of historical interest with archives where Adrian and her father might potentially go. Bernardo had spotted them at Zeyrek Mosque—and lost them. She'd tamped down her fury and ordered him to keep looking.

Before ending the call, Bernardo had sent her a photo of another man who was now with them, a former member turned traitor of the Dieci, Erasmo Aydin. Anger filled her at the sight of Erasmo; she had no patience nor tolerance for traitors. She'd ordered Bernardo to shoot him on sight once he caught him.

Getting up from the desk where she'd been seated, looking over a report from the lab, Vittoria moved across the spacious study to the balcony which overlooked the waterfront view of the Bosphorus. She was staying at the mansion of a Dieci member who was away on business. Under normal circumstances, she'd enjoy staying in such a luxurious home, but given her recent frustrations, she could hardly appreciate her accommodations.

It was also increasingly difficult just being in Istanbul, with too many flashbacks of her former life filtering in, making it difficult for her to concentrate. At least several times someone—either a member of her security team or a researcher—had to repeat her name, as she found herself drifting in the sea of memories. And she'd barely been able to sleep, her nights punctuated by nightmares.

Another flash of her husband's and son's faces appeared in her mind's eye. In one of her recurring nightmares, her husband pleaded with her to not go forward with her plans.

"This isn't who you are, Tori," he'd whispered, tears in his golden brown eyes. "You were meant to save people, not slaughter them."

"I am saving them," she'd returned, and repeated one of the Dieci's mottos. "Destruction leads to creation . . . to rebirth."

His distraught face would disappear, and she would search for him, unable to find his or her son's dead bodies in the rubble of the explosion that had taken their lives. She would wake up, shaking, sobs wracking her body.

Vittoria shoved away the pain, burying it deep, forcing herself to focus on the present and her goals. She reminded herself of the ace up her sleeve, the thing that would bring both Adrian and Robert West to heel until she could dispose of them. She just needed calm . . . and patience.

"Doctor Trivisana?"

Vittoria looked up as one of her historical researchers, Sofia, entered. Sofia was a brilliant historian based in Istanbul, and reminded Vittoria of herself when she was still in her twenties, but with none of that foolish idealism. Sofia was one of the few researchers who knew what the Dieci was truly up to, and she wholeheartedly supported it.

Sofia looked nervous as she stepped forward, handing Vittoria a document. "One of the other researchers found this. It's been in our archives in Venice for some time and was overlooked. When we examined it a second time, we realized how relevant it is to what we're looking for."

As Vittoria examined the document, her frustration melted away.

Sofia hovered, her body rigid with tension, clearly expecting Vittoria's anger. But Vittoria offered her a wide smile. She should be angered that the Dieci already had this in their archives, something that could certainly have accelerated their search for the key, but there was no time for anger now.

"Thank you," Vittoria said. Sofia's tension dissipated, her shoulders relaxing as Vittoria continued, "Tell Isabella to have the pilot prepare my plane."

Sofia nodded and dutifully left the study. As excited as Vittoria was by this new development, she was even more relieved to finally get out of this abominable city with all of its painful memories.

Destruction was the only path to rebirth, and this latest discovery would bring her one step closer to ending it all.

Bucharest, Romania
6:09 PM

POLINA DUG AROUND in her bag for the keys to her apartment, taking a quick look around at her surroundings. She'd decided to return to her apartment after another day of following Mikhail. He'd repeated the same pattern as he did yesterday, going directly from work to home, only this time she hadn't seen Florin's car or any sign of him. She had no great love for Florin, but after seeing those two imposing men, she was worried about him.

Polina honestly didn't know how she was going to move forward; she just felt safer in her apartment, where she could brainstorm what to do next. She'd thought about going to the authorities, but she didn't have any evidence for her claims, nor did she know how to get such evidence.

Despite what she'd heard, there was a large part of her that still hoped she was wrong and this was all some misunderstanding that she was reading way too much into. Yet her instincts were rarely wrong . . . and her instincts told her that Mikhail needed to be stopped.

But how?

Shaking her head with frustration, she unlocked her door, stepped inside . . . and froze in her tracks.

There were two people standing in her living room—a man and a woman around her age. The woman, a tall, willowy brunette, approached, holding up her hands to indicate she meant no harm.

"I'm sorry that we had to meet this way," she said. "I'm Adrian West with the Federal Bureau of

Investigation in the United States, and this is my partner, Nick Harper. Millions of people are in danger, and we think you can help save them."

CHAPTER 27

Doctor Polina Lysenko was a petite woman with honey blond hair and deep green eyes that shone with intelligence. She looked younger in person than in the photos they'd found of her online, seeming more like a student than a doctor, even though Adrian knew they were around the same age.

She was staring at them in shock, probably more from what Adrian had just told her than the fact that two strangers were in her apartment.

Once they'd used Erasmo's hacking skills to find out where she lived, the decision to approach Doctor Lysenko this way had been a risky one, but they'd determined it was the best method given the circumstances they were under. The institute where she worked could be compromised. Doctor Lysenko herself could be compromised, but they needed to control the environment. Robert and

Erasmo were outside in their rental car as backup, just in case they needed to make a quick escape.

"A few months ago, a research team at the institute where you work discovered a mass grave of plague victims," Adrian said, knowing that she needed to get to her point—quickly—before the other woman went into full panic mode. She studied Doctor Lysenko's face closely as she spoke. The young woman stiffened at her words, her back going ramrod straight. *She knows something.*

Adrian decided to take the risk and tell her the truth. "We're here because there's a dangerous group of people that want to release a modern day plague. There may be a link between what your team found and what they plan to do. Have you noticed anything suspicious at the institute? Anything out of the ordinary?"

Doctor Lysenko went even more pale at her words, and Adrian knew her words were resonating. Adrian took out her badge and held it up so that she could see it.

"These are our credentials. We need to stop these people, and if you know something, that can help us."

After several long moments, Doctor Lysenko held out her hand, and Adrian handed over her badge, Nick doing the same. She studied both badges for a long moment before her eyes filled with tears, her shoulders sinking with relief as she muttered something in Romanian.

"I'm not happy that you broke into my home,"

Doctor Lysenko said, "but the angels must have sent you. Everything you said makes sense." Her voice broke. "I haven't known what to do."

Adrian, her father, Nick, and Erasmo were gathered in Doctor Lysenko's—who insisted they call her Polina—study. They sipped steaming mugs of tea as Polina told them everything she'd discovered over the past few days, ending with overhearing her boss discussing the extraction of a pathogen.

This chilled Adrian to the bone, and she exchanged nervous looks with Nick and the others. Polina's words were confirming what they'd feared.

"Tell us more about the pathogen you found in the samples," Robert said, leaning forward, his brow furrowed with worry.

"Some had differing genetic material, which means different strains of pathogen, which you rarely find in mass graves of people who died of the same illness at the same time. I didn't have a chance to sequence it, but from what I could glean, the strains that differed were more virulent."

Another chill spread over Adrian's body as she realized the implication of what Polina had just told them. A *more* virulent strain of the pathogen that had caused the Black Death? This could be exactly what the Dieci was looking for.

"But the pathogen for the Black Plague still

exists today. Now we have modern medicine that can kill these bugs—even more virulent strains," Nick said.

"Well, if I were trying to engineer a modern day plague . . . " Polina said slowly, leaning back in her chair, "I would make something that could evade modern antibiotics. I would pair it with a virus. A more virulent strain of the Yersinia pestis bacterium paired with a bio-engineered virus? The results would be . . . apocalyptic."

Dread flooded Adrian at her words. She'd suspected something like this ever since she'd figured out what the Dieci wanted to do, but hearing a paleopathologist confirm it . . .

"You said this organization wants to unleash something like this onto the world?" Polina asked, her expression filling with horrified disbelief as Adrian nodded. "Mikhail—Doctor Kolov, my boss—he must be involved, then."

"What do you know about him?" Nick asked.

"He's been . . . inappropriate with me at times, how you say in English a bit of a creep, but I never would have thought him capable of mass murder," she said, shaking her head.

"Doctor Mikhail Kolov," Erasmo echoed, taking out his tablet and typing in his name. Her father stood, peering over Erasmo's shoulder. He abruptly went still at what he saw.

"Dad? What is it?" Adrian asked.

"I know him," Robert said, finally looking up from the tablet. "I've seen him meeting with the higher ups. He's a member of the Dieci or he works for them."

Polina let out a soft gasp, and Adrian turned to face her. "I don't want to scare you, but these are very dangerous people," Adrian said. "Are you able to take an extended leave of absence from work and go somewhere safe?"

Some of Polina's color returned, and she frowned. "I'm already on a fake vacation while I look into all of this. Now that I know my suspicions are true, I can't just run away. We need to get to Mikhail's lab—I believe that's where he took the samples. It's in the basement of his home. I can help get us inside."

Adrian hesitated, not wanting to bring a civilian into this, but the others looked like they were on Polina's side.

Sensing Adrian's lingering hesitation, Polina leaned forward. "You're going to need a paleopathologist on your team. I have no doubt that this organization has more than one on theirs. I can help stop them. Ever since I discovered those different strains, I became involved."

Adrian looked at Nick and the others, and they gave her nods of agreement. She turned back to Polina. "Tell us how we can get into this lab."

CHAPTER 28

9:48 PM

Adrian huddled in the bushes next to Nick and Polina outside the back door of Mikhail's home, her pulse racing with anticipation. He lived in a quiet neighborhood, and at the moment his street was mostly isolated.

She glanced over at Nick, giving him a nod to signal that it was time to act.

Nick grinned, lifting a rock that he was clutching in his hand. "There's something so satisfying about smashing things with rocks."

He stood, hurling the rock at the narrow window adjacent to the back door. As it shattered, he raced to the side of the doorway, sinking down into a crouch.

Several heartbeats later, one of the men whom Polina had told them about hurried out the door, his eyes sweeping around and his weapon at the ready. To Adrian's relief, he was alone.

Nick leapt to his feet and tackled the man to the ground from behind, before he caught Nick in his line of sight. Startled, the man attempted to twist out of Nick's grasp, but Nick yanked his weapon out of his hand and slammed it down hard onto his temple, repeatedly, until the guard stilled.

Adrian hurried forward, helping Nick drag the man's unconscious body to where they'd just been hiding by the bushes.

"Is—is he dead?" Polina hedged, stepping forward, her face pale.

"Unfortunately, no," Nick muttered. "But he's going to have a massive headache when he wakes up."

Polina slid her gaze away from the unconscious man's body, swallowing hard. Adrian knew that this was way out of her comfort zone. But much of this had been her idea, and so far it was working.

Polina had sent a threatening text to Mikhail, telling him she knew what he was up to and to meet her at the institute. He'd taken the bait and gone to the institute with one of his men, leaving behind the guard whom they'd just encountered. Erasmo was trailing Mikhail to the institute, while Robert was waiting outside in their rental, ready to whisk them away when they were ready to flee.

Polina approached the back door of Mikhail's house, trailed closely by Adrian and Nick. Her hands were shaking badly, so Adrian stepped forward to open the door by reaching in through the shattered window.

She and Nick entered first, taking out their weapons, cautiously entering a long, wood-paneled corridor, but the rooms they passed—a study, a kitchen, a dining room and a drawing room—were all empty. Nick quickly checked upstairs to make certain it was all clear before returning.

Only then did they allow Polina to lead the way, trailing her further down the corridor to a set of stairs that led to the basement, where she'd told them that Mikhail's lab was located.

They crept down the stairs, their movements cautious, before heading to the door at the end of the corridor that led to Mikhail's lab.

Adrian stiffened with alarm, raising her weapon as the door swung open. A man stumbled out, looking at them with wide, frightened eyes.

"Florin, wait—" Polina began, but he immediately turned to rush back inside the lab.

Adrian and Nick were faster. They both darted forward, Nick keeping the door open with his muscular frame. Adrian advanced toward Florin, aiming her gun at his chest. Florin put his hands up as he stumbled back, his eyes wide with panic.

"We know what you're doing here," Polina said, her expression hard as she stepped forward. "Where are the bone samples? Did you extract the pathogen?"

Florin went pale at her words, furiously shaking his head. "No, they were too badly degraded," he replied in heavily accented English. "But Mikhail still had them shipped."

Panic and hope both swelled in Adrian's chest. If he was telling the truth about the samples being too degraded, they still had time. But if he was lying, and the Dieci had extracted a deadly pathogen... they were already too late.

"Where were the samples shipped?" she demanded.

"I don't know, I swear—Mikhail wouldn't tell me," Florin stammered.

"Are you certain the samples were too badly degraded?" Polina demanded. "Do you know what these monsters are planning to do?"

"I didn't—at first. When I guessed what they were planning, I begged Mikhail to not do it. I didn't want to be a part of it, but he threatened my family," Florin said shakily. "And yes, I'm certain. We tried a sample extraction, but the material—the bone fragments—were too old and degraded to make them viable."

"If the samples weren't viable, what did he have you working on here?" Polina asked.

"He wanted to keep trying, even though I told him all the samples were in the same state. If—if he hadn't threatened my family, I swear I would not have done any of it," he said, pressing a hand to his mouth, stifling a desperate sob.

Adrian studied Florin's terrified expression. His fear was genuine, and her gut told her he was telling the truth. Still, she would feel better knowing where that sample was headed and confirmation that any pathogen extraction wasn't viable.

Her cell suddenly chimed with a text. Nick kept his weapon trained on Florin, so she reached down to her phone to check her messages. The text was from Erasmo.

> Leave—now. Mikhail and his guard are coming back to the house.

CHAPTER 29

Mikhail and his guard approached the front door, their bodies stiff with tension.

Adrian and Nick were huddled inside the foyer on opposite sides of the doorway. She could see Mikhail and his guard's approach from the small window next to the door.

They had tied up Florin in the basement, along with the unconscious guard, and Polina was hiding in the dining room.

After receiving Erasmo's text, they were initially going to take his advice and flee, but Adrian had decided against it. Mikhail would have information they desperately needed about the pathogen, information that Florin didn't have.

The guard reached the front door, Mikhail hovering a few feet behind him. He kicked it open, his gun out and at the ready as he entered.

Nick sprang into action and lunged forward, but the guard was quick, whirling to fire. Adrian stepped forward, raising her pistol and firing first, hitting the guard in the chest.

Outside, Mikhail stumbled back, his face paling as he turned to flee. But Erasmo approached him from behind with a wide grin before calmly punching him in the face.

Mikhail sank to his knees, moaning in pain, as Erasmo and Nick dragged him inside. Robert, who'd emerged from the rental car, trailed them.

They tossed Mikhail down onto the floor of the foyer as Polina emerged from the dining room. Mikhail twisted to face her, his face reddening with anger.

"Polina," he hissed. "What have you done? Why are you—"

"We ask the questions," Adrian interrupted, stepping forward and leveling her weapon at him. They had little time; his guard had likely called for backup before they'd arrived. "Where did you ship the samples?"

Mikhail swallowed, his eyes darting back and forth between all of them. "I don't know what—"

"We're not playing this game," Nick snapped. "We know all about the organization you're working for and what they're planning to do. Now, we're going to ask you again. Where were they sent?"

Mikhail remained silent, his jaw tight.

"Mikhail, please," Polina said, taking a cautious

step forward. "You know what they're planning to do is wrong. You're not a murderer. Just tell us what—"

Mikhail cursed at Polina in Romanian, spitting on her. Polina stumbled back, looking startled by his vitriol.

Erasmo let out a heavy sigh and moved forward, raising his pistol and shooting Mikhail in the thigh. Mikhail fell onto his side, clutching his thigh and letting out a howl of pain.

"I have no problem killing you," Erasmo said, his expression cold. "Answer our questions or I start shooting more body parts. Not a fun way to die, my friend."

"It—it was an address in Warsaw," Mikhail gasped as he gripped his bleeding thigh. "But it's just a drop-off location—they're very careful."

"Was the sample you extracted viable?" Nick demanded.

Mikhail hissed in pain before answering. "N—no. It was too degraded, but they wanted to study it, anyway."

"Who is your boss?" Adrian pressed. "Who do you report to?"

"I only know her first name," he bit out. "Vittoria. I—I was to meet with her in Genoa tomorrow."

"Where in Genoa?" Nick demanded.

"I—I don't know," Mikhail said. "I told you, they're very careful. They—they would have picked me up at the airport. Please—my leg—"

"Why does she want to meet you in person?

You said the sample isn't viable," Adrian interrupted.

"It isn't. I think she just wants to discuss—" Mikhail's words faltered as his face drained of color, and he slumped over, unconscious.

Erasmo rolled his eyes, looking down at Mikhail with annoyance. "That was just a flesh wound. I could have done a lot more damage. He is—what do you say in English? A pussycat," he muttered.

"Not exactly the right term, but we know what you're talking about," Nick said wryly. "We could have gotten more out of him, you know," he added, giving Erasmo an irritated look. "This is why we don't shoot people we need answers from."

Erasmo just offered a casual shrug. "You got your answers, didn't you?"

"He was telling the truth about Genoa," Polina said. "When I overheard him speaking to his two guards at the institute, they mentioned it."

"And he was probably also telling the truth about where the samples were sent," Robert added. "In my time working for them, I was never given direct addresses . . . either decoys or I was picked up directly."

Adrian stiffened when she heard sirens approaching in the distance. They could be heading somewhere else—or right their way.

Moments later, they were speeding away from the house. Polina had staunched Mikhail's wound, and they'd dragged him down to the lab, leaving him with the tied up and pleading Florin and unconscious guard. Adrian sent a text to Briggs updating him, and he'd promptly replied, telling them he would handle the mess back at Mikhail's home with the local authorities.

Adrian's thoughts turned to Mikhail's attempt at extracting the pathogen from the bone samples. "This clarifies exactly what they're looking for. A body—or bodies—that has a viable and more virulent strain of the pathogen for the Black Plague."

"That's going to be difficult," Polina said. "It's not like archaeologists are constantly finding mass graves of plague victims. Despite how any people died, finds of plague victims like the mass grave my institute discovered aren't common. And considering they're looking for a particularly virulent strain . . . "

Her words gave Adrian a small measure of hope, but not much. The Dieci were determined to find such a strain, and they had the resources to do so.

"There has to be something significant in Genoa if Vittoria is there now," Adrian said.

"Then we need to go there," her father replied. "We can start with the state archives. They'll have burial information on plague victims. It's at least a place to start."

"True. But given our encounter with Mikhail, it's only a matter of time before Vittoria knows we're onto them and they'll expect us to come to Genoa. I don't think even flying under assumed names is safe, "Adrian returned.

"If I may," Erasmo said, a mischievous gleam in his eyes. "I think I have us covered in that area."

CHAPTER 30

Terate, Italy
11:02 PM

Cora was going to escape.

She looked out the window at the dark Italian countryside, determination pulsing through her. She was alone in the farmhouse. Ivan had left an hour ago. She didn't know where he'd gone, as she'd pretended to be asleep right before he'd left. She noticed with a chill that he'd locked her bedroom door before leaving, something he hadn't done before, which convinced her even more that she needed to get the hell out of here.

Ivan had barely spoken to her, avoiding her eyes and treating her more and more like a captive than someone he was trying to protect. She'd used his distance to her advantage, subtly sacking away supplies into a makeshift getaway bag; she'd even found a couple of hundred euros tucked away in a drawer in one of the empty rooms.

Her plan was to head into town and hire a local to take her to the American embassy in Milan. She knew it was risky, but something had shifted with Ivan, and she no longer felt safe here with him. She could figure out further steps once she was at the embassy, but first she was going to get the hell out of here.

Time to execute the plan, she told herself after scanning the horizon for what seemed like the millionth time for Ivan's return.

But just as she was about to grab her hastily packed bag, she saw the headlights of a car approaching in the distance. The sleek black Audi wasn't Ivan's rental, and it was headed directly toward the farmhouse.

The Audi came to a stop directly in front of the farmhouse; Cora watched with dread as a man and a woman emerged. She stumbled back from the window, instinctively knowing they were here for her.

Grabbing her bag, she darted to the back window of the bedroom, thanking every god she could think of that the bedroom was on the ground floor. She pushed it open with all her might—thankfully Ivan had overlooked this window when he'd locked her inside. Using all her strength, she hefted herself out of the window, landing in an undignified heap on the ground before taking off at a sprint.

Cora wasn't nearly as athletic as her daughter, but she ran as fast as she could, even as she heard shouts behind her, ordering her to stop in English—which only caused her to pick up her pace.

She knew they would be able to catch up with her, it was only a matter of time. Cora took an abrupt left, veering off into the trees, her heart in her throat as she ran, searching for a place to hide.

She hadn't gone twenty feet when a large male body tackled her to the ground from behind. Panicked, she struggled to release herself until she heard a familiar voice.

"Cora. *Stop*."

She froze, turning to face Ivan. "Do not fight them. You are more valuable to them alive, but they will not hesitate to hurt you."

Cora stared at him, blinking back tears. Even though she'd only known him for two days and was planning an escape, the betrayal she felt was still like a gut punch. Deep down, she'd hoped she'd been wrong about him.

"I am sorry," he continued, giving her a look of regret. "You were right about my son. I had sent him away, but they found him. They will kill him if I do not cooperate. Just—please. Play along."

With that, he roughly grabbed her arm, yanking her to her feet as the man and woman approached. They exchanged words in Italian before the man stepped forward, taking her arm and pulling her away from Ivan.

Despair filled Cora as they dragged her to their car.

I'm sorry Robert. I'm sorry Adrian. My loves. I tried.

～

Airspace over the Black Sea
6:32 AM

Adrian looked down at the rippling waters of the Black Sea below, the steady hum of the plane's engines calming her nerves.

Erasmo had a contact that had proven invaluable. They'd driven two and a half hours to an airstrip near the Russian border, where they'd boarded a private plane. For a hefty fee that they'd arranged for the task force to pay, Erasmo's contact, a Russian pilot named Sergey, had agreed to take them to Genoa, and at least one more destination after that—within reason.

Since that stroke of good luck, however, they'd received a series of bad news. Briggs had reached out to inform them he had no information on Vittoria. Whoever she was, she kept a low profile. There was also no news on the location of Lucija Novak, nor had the local authorities in Dubrovnik been able to identify the shooter.

The authorities in Bucharest hadn't been as forthcoming, not giving him any further information on the men at Mikhail's home, or the current status of Mikhail or Florin. Their reticence could simply mean that they didn't like having to answer to American law enforcement—or they were linked to the Dieci.

And shortly after hearing from Briggs, Erasmo's contact had gotten back to him about her father's friend Oliver . . . he'd been found dead. The Dieci had gotten to him.

At her side, her father was quiet, still reeling from news of Oliver's death, gazing out the window with a hollow expression.

"Dad . . . I'm sorry about Oliver," Adrian murmured.

"He gave me hope when for so long I had none," Robert said, closing his eyes. "I was too afraid to even look you or your mother up online that first year. I was terrified that they'd gotten to you both and killed you anyway. Ollie was the one who got me images of you and your mother. It was those images that made me determined to get away from the Dieci and back to the both of you."

He paused for a long moment, raking his hand through his hair. "Ollie admitted he made mistakes using his hacking skills to help the wrong people. But he was trying so desperately to get away from the Dieci, to get on the right side of the law. And now he'll never be able to." His voice hardened with anger. "They've taken the life of another good man. Another friend. I can't let them get away with this."

"You won't," Adrian said, determination of her own swelling. "*We* won't."

Robert met her eyes, and his expression softened. He smiled, his gaze finding Nick, who was seated several rows ahead of them, speaking in hushed tones with Erasmo and Polina. "I know that now may not be the time for this, and you don't need my blessing, but if I've learned anything . . . I know that life is short. I want you to know I approve of Nick. It's clear how much he loves you."

Adrian returned his smile, following his gaze to Nick, warmth coursing through her. It surprised her how much her father's words meant to her. "He's wonderful. But don't tell him that. He'll get a big head," she added with a light chuckle. "When you get to know him, you'll like him even more."

She realized this was the first time she'd hinted at a future relationship with her father. Since he'd reappeared in her life, her focus had solely been on stopping the Dieci.

She tentatively allowed herself to envision a future with her father in it, making up for lost time. Dinners with Nick and her mother. Visits to her apartment in DC. When he was ready, introducing him to the task force. Helping him reintegrate back into society after being held captive for so long.

"When this is all over, we have a lot of time to make up for, sweetheart," Robert said, seeming to read her mind. His voice wavered as he continued, "I'll forever regret the years spent away from you and your mother. I wish I had found a way back to you sooner."

"You did what you had to do," Adrian said. "I understand that now."

And she did. Now that she had encountered two branches of this secret society, she knew how deadly they were, how terrified her father must have been for her and her mother.

"We need to think about what exactly we're looking for once we get to Genoa," Adrian said.

"I've been mulling over the Genoa aspect of all this, ever since you mentioned back in Istanbul it being no coincidence that the Genoans, enemies of the Venetians, were the ones who transported the plague into Italy. I wasn't sure how it connected until Polina told us about the more virulent strain found in the mass grave. I think a doctor sympathetic to the Venetians, perhaps even a Venetian himself, was working in Kaffa at the time. When the siege hits the city by the Mongol army and they begin committing biological warfare, I think he saw an opportunity. As I've said before, doctors may not have known about germs, but they did know about infectiousness. I think this doctor purposefully exposed Genoan merchants, maybe under the guise of treating them, to the more virulent strains of the pathogen. The Genoans returned to Italy . . . and the rest is history."

As Adrian considered his words, Erasmo's alarmed voice interrupted her thoughts. "Robert. Adrian."

Adrian and her father looked up. Erasmo was approaching them, looking shaken, trailed by an equally shaken Nick and Polina. He was holding up one of his phones.

"I've been monitoring your emails since we found out about Oliver—I had access to his security logins. This link just came in from Vittoria to the last email address you were using for the Dieci."

Erasmo held out the phone, and terror rocked Adrian to her core.

On the screen was a live video of her mother, bound and gagged, a pistol pressed to the side of her head, tears streaming down her face.

CHAPTER 31

Genoa, Italy
6:59 AM

When Vittoria's cell phone rang, she already knew who was on the other end. She'd included a phone number at the bottom of the 'message' she'd sent to Robert West.

She answered using the video option, smiling at the furious faces of Robert and Adrian West on her screen.

"I see you got my message," Vittoria said cooly.

"Where is she?!" Adrian snarled. "What have you—"

"There is no time for this back and forth," Vittoria said with a dismissive wave of her hand. "If you want to see Cora West again, *alive*, you will meet me here in Genoa."

Moments later, after Vittoria had relayed her instructions and ended the call, she leaned back in her chair, allowing a satisfied smile to curl her lips. After a series of frustrating setbacks, things were finally moving in a positive direction.

Back in Istanbul, the document that Sofia had given her was a coded letter found in the Dieci's archives in Venice, a letter that had previously been overlooked. So far, they had only decoded a handful of words, but they were enough to determine that it referred to the key they were looking for.

She had forced Ivan Vasiliev, a former bodyguard who'd once worked for the Dieci and turned traitor, to bring in Cora West by threatening his son's life. Cora was useful bait for now; once Vittoria used Adrian and Robert West's skills to help them decode the letter, she would eliminate all the Wests in one fell swoop.

Still smiling, she looked out the grand windows of her private office that overlooked the lush gardens of the inner courtyard.

She was in her childhood home, a villa that had been in her family for generations, a place her ancestors had christened with the title *Villa Dell'Amore,* home of love. Villa Dell'Amore was located in the wealthy Albaro district, near the historic center of the city. Once a holiday retreat for well-to-do Genoese, villas from the height of Genoa's wealthy past still dotted the district. An ancestor of hers was a Venetian who had married a Genoan when Italy was still divided into warring factions, and though it had been controversial at the time, the marriage united the Genoese and Venetian sides of her family.

Vittoria was relieved to be in Genoa. It didn't hold the painful memories that Istanbul conjured. Her childhood had truly been one of love when her father was still alive. He would walk hand in hand with her through the many rooms of the villa, telling her stories of all the generations of her family who'd once lived here. Her cousins would visit often, and they would chase each other throughout the villa, taking advantage of its infinite hiding places.

When she became interested in biology and medicine as a teen, she would spend hours in the study, perusing all the books her family had collected over generations on the subject. She couldn't wait to go to medical school to change the world for the better.

How naïve she had been. This world couldn't be made better; the only hope for it was to start anew.

"Vittoria."

She turned. Isabella hovered in the doorway. Vittoria frowned; the Wests couldn't possibly be here yet. She'd made them tell her exactly where they were; they had coincidentally been on their way to Genoa. They had to be at her front door by one PM Central European Time sharp, or she would kill Cora West.

"They're not here yet," Isabella said, reading her mind. "I just wanted you to know that I reached out to the other leaders on your behalf to let them know about the letter, like you asked."

Vittoria gave her a nod; she hated dealing with the other leaders directly but felt the need to let them know she was making some progress. Isabella turned to leave, but hesitated. She turned back to face her.

"I hope you find the key ... and soon. Some of the things I saw when I served in the military ... "

Her dark eyes shadowed, a haunted look flickering across her face. Vittoria knew Isabella had a military background before she went into the private security sector; she had served two tours in both Iraq and Afghanistan. "Humanity cannot be saved. *Dalla distruzione alla rinascita.*"

Destruction to rebirth. Vittoria smiled, echoing her words, "*Dalla distruzione alla rinascita.*"

By the time the Wests arrived at the villa several hours later, Vittoria was feeling even more resolute, Isabella's words lighting a fire in her belly. She made her way downstairs and into the grand foyer as Isabella, Bernardo, and another one of her guards dragged Adrian, Nick, and Robert inside. Vittoria could tell that Adrian was trying to maintain her calm, but she saw the barely contained loathing in the other woman's eyes.

"Vittoria, please," Robert said, stepping forward. "I know the consequences for what I've done, and I'll accept whatever punishment you see fit. But please, let my wife and daughter—"

"You've always known what the price of

betrayal would be. But . . . you have one last opportunity to save yourself, and your family," she lied.

Adrian's expression didn't change, but her father's filled with hope. Vittoria turned to one of her guards, ordering him in Italian to take Nick down to the cellars. Adrian watched him go, worry and fear in her eyes. For a split second, a pang of envy pierced Vittoria. She had loved her husband that much and lost him anyway.

"If you cooperate, you'll see him again—and Cora," Vittoria snapped. She turned to head toward the study; Isabella and Bernardo dragging the two Wests after her.

Once inside the study, Vittoria gestured to copies of the letter that she'd placed on the central table.

"The price of Cora West's life," she said. "You will decode this letter, and you will do it swiftly."

AFTER VITTORIA LEFT them in the study, Adrian picked up the copy of the letter, anxiety filling her.

Unlike the letter they'd discovered in Dubrovnik, this one was longer and more complex, several pages long, with many more symbols and hardly any letters, which would make it even more difficult to decode. How was she and her father alone—in a short amount of time—supposed to decode something that would typically take trained professionals weeks, if not months?

Vittoria must have a team of researchers working for her. Why did she need them? This had to just be busy work before the inevitable. Despite Vittoria's promises, Adrian knew she had no intentions of letting them or her mother go. The Dieci had wanted to kill her since before she'd come onto this case, and her father had betrayed them.

They needed to buy time for their escape attempt.

After Vittoria had contacted them on the plane, they had come up with a hasty plan. When Vittoria demanded they tell her where they were, she had asked about Erasmo. Adrian had lied and told her that he was back in Istanbul. Vittoria had seemed to buy that—at least for now. Fortunately, Vittoria also didn't know that Polina was with them, which they used to their advantage.

Erasmo had told Adrian and Robert to get themselves taken to a second location, and he would take it from there. Adrian was hesitant, not wanting to put her mother's life in danger, but this was the best option they had to free themselves and track her mother down.

She glanced over at her father, who looked pale with fear as he studied the letter. He was even more of an expert in ancient documents than she was and must know this would be impossible to decode in a timely manner.

"We should start by classifying the symbols," she said out loud, for the sake of the guard who was in the study with them.

She reached down to one of two notebooks that Vittoria had left on the table for them, and jotted down a quick message in Arabic, a language she hoped her captors didn't know. Her father glanced down at it and gave her the subtlest of nods. He was on board with her plan.

Adrian set down the copies of the letter in between them, and together they got to work.

CHAPTER 32

Unknown

Cora sat huddled in the darkened cellar, the binds of the zip ties digging into painfully into her wrists, the gag around her mouth making her feel claustrophobic. She wasn't sure how long she'd been in here; thus far she'd been fed two meager meals that consisted only of bread and water.

At some point her captors had entered the cellar, with one of them placing the barrel of a gun against her temple while the other one filmed her with a cell phone camera. Terror had flooded Cora as she gazed at the camera, certain that she was going to die.

Moments from her life flickered in her mind's eye—her idyllic childhood in Maryland, her attempt at rebellion during her teen years, bumping into Robert during her freshman year in college and falling instantly, helplessly in love, the soul-changing joy that washed over her when she'd held the newborn Adrian in her arms.

But after a few harrowing moments, her captor had lowered his weapon, and they'd both left her alone, shaking and petrified, tears streaming down her face.

Now, Cora leaned her head against the wall, taking in a shuddering breath. She had no idea how Adrian routinely dealt with situations like these. It was why Cora hadn't wanted her to join the FBI in the first place, especially after what happened to her father.

Adrian had never given her explicit details of her work with the bureau, knowing how worried she would be, but Cora could only guess. The reality was worse than even Cora could have predicted.

What if her captors came back and executed her this time? Fear spiked in her chest, and she again forced herself to calm down by taking multiple deep breaths. She began to methodically to work at the zip ties around her wrists, using her wedding band as friction. Even after holding a funeral for Robert she could never bring herself to take it off.

Cora had been working at the zip ties off and on since she'd been dragged down here, and had made very little—if any—progress. But it still felt like she was accomplishing something, even if it was a small something. She wasn't going to just sit here and let these bastards kill her. She was determined to at least try to see her daughter and husband again.

Cora paused her efforts against the zip ties as she heard a commotion outside of the cellar—it sounded like it was coming from above.

She stilled, straining her ears to listen. She heard muffled shouts, and then several gunshots. Fear tore through her as she heard steady footsteps descend the stairs and approach the cellar.

Shaking, she stumbled to her feet, moving to the opposite side of the door. *Much of self defense is the element of surprise,* Adrian had once told her. She held her breath as the footsteps moved closer. Keys rattled in the door, and as soon as it burst open on its hinges—

Cora lunged forward, intending to tackle whoever entered, but she only ran into a solid wall of muscle. Terror coursed through her as she looked up, but it instantly vanished when she saw that it was Ivan.

"I am sorry it took me so long," Ivan said, holding his hands up to indicate he meant no harm. "I had to make certain my son was safe before I attempted to rescue you. We have to go. Now."

Cora stared at him, doubt and uncertainty swirling in her mind. Ivan stepped forward, extending his hand. "I know it is hard to trust me now, and you can hate me, but we have to go—now. They will be sending backup."

Cora finally nodded. *The devil you know.* She

certainly didn't want to see what her captors' backup was like.

Ivan took out a knife, and she jerked back, but he just sliced off her zip ties and gag. "Come on. We need to run."

He turned, and she followed him, racing up the stairs. They were in a small cottage; her two captors were on the floor of the entranceway, dead. Nausea rose in Cora's gut and she averted her gaze, trailing Ivan as he kept moving. He made his way out the back door, where an old Fiat awaited them behind the cottage.

"Are you OK?" Ivan asked, continually checking the rear-view mirror as he sped away from the cottage moments later. "Did they hurt you?"

Cora shook her head. "I'm fine," she said shakily. "How—how did they find us? Did you—"

"The men sent by the Dieci who were going to abduct you tracked me going into your home right before we escaped. Not long after we got to the farmhouse, the Dieci reached out to me and threatened my son if I did not reveal my location and where you were." He shook his head with regret. "You were right . . . I never wanted to be part of the Dieci. They used my son as leverage, the way they used you and your daughter against Robert. It is how they operate. And they do not make empty threats."

A chill spread throughout Cora's body. "Your son—"

"They cannot get to my son. I made certain of

it. I will get you somewhere safe. We are still in Italy, not far from Milan. We need to get out of this country, maybe go to—"

"No," Cora interrupted. "We'll find my daughter and husband and join them. I'm no longer going to be a sitting duck. If these people capture me again, they're just going to use me for leverage and probably kill me this time."

Ivan studied her for a long moment, a look of admiration on his face.

"What?"

"Remember when you told me you do not know where your daughter gets her bravery from? I see exactly where she gets it from."

Genoa, Italy
1:57 PM

ADRIAN STARED down at the letter, frustration coursing through her.

For the past few hours she and her father had pored over it, trying to make sense of the series of symbols and few words interspersed throughout. Vittoria had at least left them a small list of words that her team had already decoded. Her team had determined that it was a letter from a Venetian spy who was in Genoa during the early days of the outbreak, and referenced a doctor secretly working on behalf of the Venetians in the city.

Adrian had planned to provide a false decoding of a part of the letter, something that would buy them much needed time and give them an excuse to go to another location. But the false information needed to be feasible, something Vittoria's team couldn't easily debunk.

Yet so far, she and her father had come up empty. Fear gripped her as she thought of her mother and Nick. They needed to come up with something, and fast.

Her father's voice pierced the panicked haze of her thoughts. "Adrian. Take a look at this."

She glanced over at her father. For the past twenty minutes, he'd been focused on one section of the letter in particular, one of the few that had words interspersed in between the symbols. He tapped a finger over the symbols.

"I've seen this before in other coded letters. I think there's a name buried here."

Adrian looked down at the letter, studying the symbols. There were several of them; a lily, a winged lion, a dove, a tree, a key, and a horse. In between the symbols were two Latin words, *USUPARE* and *MORS*, which meant 'usurper' and 'death'.

She suspected the key symbol was significant, and she knew the winged lion referred to Venice, as it was the symbol of Saint Mark, the city's patron saint. But other than that . . .

"I'm not seeing a pattern," she said.

"It's like a code within a code," Robert said.

"Whoever wrote this letter didn't want this to be easy to decode. I suspect these two Latin words refer to a name—they're written together three times throughout the letter. I think that's significant."

Adrian studied the other two places where the same Latin words were written. The letters were in the same order, but the symbols differed, and Adrian could now see what her father was referring to. The symbols that surrounded the letters seemed to be there as a way to throw off anyone looking for a pattern. The words were probably what was important.

"*Usupare* and *mors*," Adrian said. "Usurper of death?"

"I think so," Robert said. "And then there's the key symbol wherever these two words are."

"So the key is the usurper of death," Adrian said slowly.

Her father nodded. She stared down at the words, hope rising in her chest. It was a good start . . . enough to carry out her plan.

"Well, we've just decoded these two words, and they refer to a name," she said, giving him a long and meaningful look. He gave her a nod, indicating that he understood the ruse and that he was following along with her plan.

On the plane during the flight to Genoa, after Vittoria's call, Adrian had forced aside her panic to read up on as much Genoan history as she could online, memorizing some Genoan family names for reference. Now, one of those names sprang to mind, like a beacon of light in pitch black darkness.

"I have a name," she said. "We need to talk to Vittoria."

Adrian looked over at the guard who was in the room with them, but at this point, he was barely paying attention to them and looked bored out of his mind. She was just about to ask him to send for Vittoria when she heard a loud, frustrated cry just outside of the study, and fierce cursing in Italian. It was Vittoria's voice.

The guard went stiff, suddenly on sharp alert. Adrian strained her ears, listening carefully to Vittoria's rapid Italian. She couldn't catch everything, but from the few words Adrian picked up, she got the gist. She closed her eyes, relief washing over her.

Her mother had escaped.

CHAPTER 33

*A*drian forced her expression to remain neutral, though she wanted to shout for joy. She glanced over at her father, who had also gone still, and she could see the same hope she felt in his eyes.

The door to the study banged open and Vittoria stormed in, her eyes wild with rage. She wasn't nearly as smug as she'd been a few hours ago, and Adrian felt a surge of pride for her mother. But she wasn't going to give any indication that she knew a key part of Vittoria's leverage was now gone.

"You've had several hours," Vittoria barked. "What have you found?"

"It would take weeks for us to fully decode this, and I think you know that," Adrian returned. "But we did find something. I want to speak to my mother before we show you what it is."

If Adrian had any doubt before that her mother had escaped, the brief look of panic that flickered across Vittoria's face before she shielded it was all the confirmation she needed. Another burst of relief filled her, but she kept her expression firm.

"You don't get to make any demands," Vittoria finally snapped. "Tell me what you have found."

"A name," Adrian said. "Vincitori. The Vincitoris were an old and powerful Genoan merchant family. We determined that these two Latin words mean usurper of death—victory over death. The word 'vincitor' in Italian means conqueror, and one of the symbols that appears next to the words is a dove, which was on the Vincitori family crest."

Adrian watched Vittoria's face carefully. Her face was a stone mask, but she seemed intrigued. Good. That was all they needed.

"We know you're looking for a body to extract the pathogen," Adrian continued. There was no point in pretending they didn't know what the Dieci were up to. "The poor were usually buried in mass graves; it's unlikely that you'll find a body with the virulent strain of pathogen that you're looking for—and samples found in mass graves are often badly degraded, like the Feodosia sample. You need to find the body of a wealthy person with this strain, someone who was buried somewhere you can access. From what your team has found already and this name, we think this letter could refer to a member of the Vincitori family who died of this strain of plague. We need to go to the Palazzo Ducale next to confirm."

Vittoria frowned. "The Doge's palace? Why?"

The Palazzo Ducale was the residence of the doge in Genoa during the medieval era. It now served as a major tourist attraction of the city that held many cultural events throughout the year. It was where Erasmo had suggested they get themselves taken to, as it was several kilometers away from Vittoria's villa, providing a window of escape.

If all else failed and he couldn't rescue them while they were in transit, there were underground tunnels at the palazzo not open to the public that they could use to escape. They were to use the historical archives at the palazzo as their excuse.

"Information about the burial places of prominent Genoese families are kept in the archives there," Adrian said now. She evenly held Vittoria's gaze, keeping her face calm though her pulse was racing. Everything hinged on Vittoria's response. She could just have someone else go to the Palazzo Ducale and keep them here, or she could just kill them and follow up on their lead on her own.

"We'll go to the Palazzo Ducale," Vittoria said finally, but she leaned in close to Adrian, her expression ice cold. "If you are lying to me? I will slit your father's throat in front of you."

3:37 *PM*

ADRIAN, her father, and to her relief, Nick, were all herded into the back of an SUV along with

Vittoria, her female guard, and the guard who'd been with them in the study.

As the SUV pulled away from Vittoria's villa, fear and adrenaline coursed through Adrian, Vittoria's threat still fresh in her mind. *I will slit your father's throat.* Panic clogged her throat, and she willed herself to calm, determination chasing away her fear. She wouldn't let Vittoria touch her father.

Once they left the affluent Albaro district, the SUV entered the Foce district, filled with parks and markets next to Genoa's busy port. Adrian was barely taking in their surroundings, her mind racing with possible ways they could escape if Erasmo couldn't get to them while in transit. But his rescue would be the best option. *Come on, Erasmo,* she thought. *Come on.*

As their driver turned onto a small side street that would take them out of the Foce district, Adrian's prayers were answered, because a car rammed into the SUV from behind, sending Adrian, Nick and her father hurtling forward.

CHAPTER 34

The force of the impact hurled Adrian, her father and Nick from the passenger seat to floor of SUV.

The SUV swerved, its tires screeching as it made a nearly three hundred and sixty degree turn in the middle of the street before slamming into two parked cars.

Pain shot up Adrian's side as she landed hard on the floor, but she gritted her teeth and ignored it, stiffening with panic as several gunshots rang out.

But the bullets weren't hitting the windows or any part of the SUV that could strike the passengers. The SUV suddenly began to rock and lower to the ground, as if being pushed down by a giant's hands, and Adrian realized that whoever was shooting had hit the tires.

Erasmo, she realized, her heart soaring with relief.

She quickly took stock of the situation. Her

father and Nick were visibly dazed, wincing with pain on the floor of the SUV alongside her, but they otherwise looked fine. The driver was slumped over the steering wheel, unconscious, having hit his head on it from the force of the collision.

The collision had hurled Vittoria and both of her guards to the right side of the SUV, and though they too look dazed, they were unfortunately conscious, slowly gathering their bearings and sitting up.

Adrian and Nick moved at the same time.

Nick lunged for the male bodyguard, taking him by surprise as he knocked the gun from his hand.

Adrian lurched toward Vittoria, who was reaching for her own weapon. Adrian dodged her female guard and punched Vittoria in the face, the act incredibly satisfying. Vittoria's hands flew up to her face with a pained grunt, and Adrian took the opportunity to grab Vittoria's pistol, raising it to fire—

But Vittoria's guard kicked the gun out of Adrian's hand, sending her hurling back against the opposite seat in the process. As she caught her breath, reeling from the blow, the guard dragged Vittoria out of the SUV, using her body to cover Vittoria from more gunshots that rang out, twisting to return fire.

Nick and her father were both struggling with the second guard, who had managed to recover his weapon. But the guard was ferociously strong, and he raised his pistol, pulling the trigger.

Nick twisted away as the bullet struck the roof of the SUV, and this time Adrian lunged forward, grabbing the guard's arm and again knocking the gun out of his hand. With a snarl, the guard reached for her throat and squeezed. Adrian gasped, struggling to breathe—

"Get your goddamned hands off my daughter!"

Adrian's father reached out and yanked the guard's arm away from her, twisting it backward until it let out a sickening crack, and the guard howled with pain. Nick grabbed his gun, shooting the guard as someone jerked open the door of the SUV.

Adrian whirled, on sharp alert, but to her relief, it was Erasmo. He gave them a roguish smile.

"Just another day at the office," he said with a wink. "I scared away the villainess and her henchwoman, but I have no doubt that backup is coming. We have to get the hell out of here."

Right on cue, she heard tires squealing as another car approached the side street.

Adrian, Nick and her father scrambled out of the SUV. They darted toward the opposite end of the street, ducking as shots rang out.

Adrian whirled; it was Vittoria and her female guard, both of whom had emerged from an empty building where they must have been hiding until backup arrived. The guard stood protectively in front of Vittoria, firing at them.

The car they'd heard, the backup car, now turned onto the side street with screeching tires, stopping behind Erasmo's car, which was blocking the path forward.

"Go!" Erasmo shouted, turning to return fire at Vittoria's guard. "Get to the end of the street—Polina will meet you there!"

Erasmo fired again, striking the female guard in the chest. Vittoria let out a cry of rage, lifting her own pistol to fire, and as Erasmo turned to race after them, her bullet struck Erasmo in his shoulder.

Erasmo staggered; Adrian and Robert darted back to grab him and help him forward as Nick turned, firing at Vittoria, who dodged his bullets by crouching down.

Another car pulled up to the opposite end of the street, and panic flooded Adrian's veins—they were trapped. Relief chased away the panic when she saw that the driver was Polina. She looked terrified, but opened the doors for them, shouting at them to hurry.

Vittoria fired again, and Nick whirled to return fire, but she once again dodged. They continued toward Polina's car, helping Erasmo into the backseat before getting in themselves. Polina floored the accelerator, racing away from the scene.

Erasmo was leaning back, his breathing ragged with pain. She and Nick lifted his shirt, examining his wound; it looked like the bullet had gone clean through, but there was a terrifying amount of blood soaking the seat around him. Nick took off his own shirt and pressed it to Erasmo's wound, causing him to hiss in pain.

"If today is my day to go to paradise, stop these bastards," Erasmo rasped, his face pale.

"Stop being so dramatic," Robert said, turning in the passenger's seat to glare back at his friend. "And don't forget, you promised we were going to get out of the Dieci together. You will not go dying on me now."

Erasmo weakly held up his middle finger. "Don't tell me what to do, you old bastard."

"You need a hospital," Adrian said, studying Erasmo's wound with concern.

"Take me to a hospital here and I'm dead. The Dieci are all over Genoa, just like Venice," Erasmo rasped. "There's an extensive first aid kit on the plane. Sergey is a bastard who's used to getting shot at."

"Fine. But we're getting you proper medical care once we land—and you better not die before then," Robert said. His eyes strayed to Adrian, filled with worry. "Where are we going?"

Ever since they'd partially decoded the letter back at Vittoria's villa, Adrian had known where they needed to go. It was a place her gut told her they were always going to return to.

"Back to where it all started," Adrian said, meeting her father's eyes. "Venice."

CHAPTER 35

Airspace over Ottone, Italy
5:58 PM

"The bleeding has stopped, for now, but he still needs proper treatment to avoid infection—and he might need a transfusion," Polina said.

Erasmo was sprawled out on two seats in the back of Sergey's private plane, where Polina had tended to him using the extensive first aid kit stowed on the plane. Though Polina was not a medical doctor, she fortunately knew enough about human anatomy to tend to a gunshot wound. Erasmo was unconscious yet stable, but Adrian knew Polina was right. He needed proper medical care.

"When we land in Venice, you and Sergey need to get him to a clinic on the mainland," Adrian said. "You've done enough to help us, and the danger is only going to intensify from here. This is the best way you can help us."

She feared Polina would protest, but after a hesitant beat, she gave Adrian a nod. Adrian turned to her father, who was hovering next to Nick, gazing down at Erasmo with concern. She knew he was worried on two fronts, just as she was—both about her mother and Erasmo.

Shortly after they had gotten on the plane and Polina had stabilized Erasmo, he'd called the number he had for Ivan, but the phone hadn't even rung.

"I know how Erasmo comes off . . . but he has a big heart. He's been a rock through all this. Just like with Ollie, he encouraged me over the years to keep fighting, insisting that I would get back to you and your mother. The Dieci . . . they had his partner killed. He doesn't show it, but I know he still has deep pain and guilt over what happened. It's been his life's mission ever since to take them down."

Adrian looked down at Erasmo, her heart filling with sympathy. She recalled the pain on his face when he'd told them about his background in Istanbul. Overall, Erasmo hid his pain well, and his determination made all the more sense now. This was personal for him.

They moved away from where Erasmo was resting, taking their seats near the front of the plane. "Venice," Robert said, turning to face Adrian. "You're certain that what we're looking for is there?"

"The clues were all there in the letter. I have some ideas about the name—usurper of death. What names mean usurper—or supplanter—of death? One common name is James; it means supplanter of death in Hebrew. The Italian version of James is Giacamo or Jacomo. As for the second name . . . I think it's been hiding in plain sight all along. We kept seeing the symbol of a key next to the two words, so I think it literally means key in Italian, which is *chiave*. There are variations of that last name in Italian—Chiave itself, Chiaveno, Chiavena, etcetera. That's who I think we're looking for . . . some form of the name Giacomo or Jacomo Chiave. You were right, Dad. The name was hidden amongst the symbols, which were basically decoys. Except for one symbol in particular."

"Which symbol?" Nick asked.

"The winged lion symbol that appeared alongside the two words. That's the symbol of Saint Mark, Venice's patron saint. It's referring to Venice. The key—the usurper of death, this Jacomo or Giacomo—is in Venice. That's where we'll find his body."

"How do you think this all links to that letter in Dubrovnik?" her father asked. "The one referring to a doctor working on a poison in Istanbul? That was written almost two centuries before the Black Death."

"I've been thinking about that as well," Adrian said. "The Black Plague wasn't the first plague that hit Europe, but it was the most devastating. There was plenty of time for doctors who were members of the Dieci to test infectiousness as a sort of biological warfare. This knowledge was passed down through generations of doctors who belonged to the Dieci, all the way down to the key—this doctor."

"I think this doctor was in Kaffa at the time of the Mongol army siege," Adrian continued. "He sees his opportunity and exposes Genoese patients to this more infectious strain under the guise of treating them. But his plan backfires. The strain is far more lethal and infectious than he intends, and it strikes down more than just the enemies of Venice—it hits Venice as well. He eventually dies of it as well. His body is preserved and knowledge of its location—and this lethal strain it carries—is lost with time."

They fell silent, considering her words. Robert started to say something, but the sound of a cell phone's ring interrupted him. They stilled.

The ringing came from one of Erasmo's many phones, which were stowed on one of the back seats of the plane.

Robert was the first to get to the ringing phone, putting it on speaker as he answered.

"Hello?"

"Oh, thank God. Robert . . . it's me."

Joy arose in Adrian's chest; she nearly staggered with relief.

It was her mother's voice.

CHAPTER 36

Venice, Italy
8:12 PM

Cora froze as she saw her husband approaching in the near distance, like a mirage come to life. Ivan hovered at her side, but she was only aware of the man she thought she'd never see again.

They were approaching the Chiesa di San Francesco della Vigna in the Castello district of Venice. They'd chosen this as a rendezvous spot because it was in the quieter part of the city, with plenty of tucked away streets and alleys to duck into in case they needed to make a quick escape. But the prospect of danger was far from Cora's mind as she took in her husband. Her living, breathing husband.

Cora and Ivan had driven from the outskirts of Milan to Venice, the drive taking longer than usual since Ivan frequently got off the motorway to take side streets east to avoid any potential pursuer.

During the drive, Cora's anger toward him had dissolved when he'd told her how the Dieci had kidnapped his son, Anton, from his school in Moscow, threatening to kill the nine-year-old unless Ivan complied. It was only when a trusted contact of his had gotten Anton to safety that he'd felt confident enough to rescue her. As a parent, Cora understood why he'd complied—the same reason she understood why Robert had sacrificed his life for their daughter.

They'd tried every number that Ivan had for both Robert and Erasmo. It was one of Erasmo's numbers that had connected, and Cora had nearly wept with relief at the sound of her husband and daughter's voices. They'd agreed to meet in Venice, not wanting to be apart any longer. She'd feared that Robert and Adrian would once again insist that she go into hiding, but to her relief, they hadn't. She sensed they didn't want to be apart any more than she did.

Now, Cora halted in her tracks, turbulent emotions swelling to the surface, and tears pricked at her eyes. So much had happened the past few days . . . fleeing from her home, learning Robert was still alive, her abduction. But this level of emotion was almost too much, and she swayed on her feet.

Her husband, though older, was just as handsome as she'd remembered, and all the memories they'd shared over the years washed over her. Their first meeting, their wedding day, their mutual tears when Adrian was born, the fights—both petty and large, the vacations, the dinners. The mundane. The exciting. Moments she'd gone over multiple times as she'd processed her grief.

Unable to stand still any longer, Cora broke into a run, and Robert hurried forward as well. He held her as she wept, and she leaned in to him. This solid, living form of *him*. Her husband. Her other half.

She pulled back as Adrian approached, tears shining in her hazel eyes as well. Nick and Ivan hovered several yards away, knowing they needed this moment as a family. Cora turned and pulled her daughter into an embrace as well, relief like she had never known flooding her.

"Are you all right, Cora?" Robert asked, his voice husky with emotion, his eyes raking over her. "Did they hurt you? How did they find you?"

Cora stiffened, her eyes inadvertently shifting to Ivan. They hadn't yet mentioned specific details of her abduction to Robert; Ivan insisted he wanted to be the one to tell him what he had done and why. Guilt flickered in Ivan's dark eyes as Cora glanced at him, and Robert's face contorted with rage; he seemed to understand instantly what had happened.

Robert lunged forward, grabbing Ivan by the collar and slamming him against the wall. Ivan was much larger than Robert, but he didn't attempt to defend himself.

"You son of a bitch," Robert snarled. "What did you do? I trusted you! You promised to—"

"Robert—stop it!" Cora cried, taking him by the arm and pushing him away from Ivan. "He had no choice. They threatened his son. And as soon as he could, *he* was the one to rescue me. He did exactly what you've been doing for the past ten years—protect his family."

Some of Robert's anger seemed to ebb at her words, but the sense of betrayal in his expression lingered.

"I am sorry," Ivan said gruffly. "They had Anton. I had no choice."

Robert closed his eyes, his shoulders sinking as his remaining anger seemed to dissipate. He took a breath, looking around at their surroundings with unease. "We shouldn't hang out in the open like this."

"Already on it," Nick said, taking out his phone.

10:37 PM

"Keep me posted," Briggs said, his expression tight with concern. "I mean it."

"Understood," Adrian said before logging off the video call. She turned to Nick with a wary smile. "I swear he's starting to sound like my actual father every day."

"Briggs is a pain in the ass, as you know, but he cares," Nick returned with a grin.

They were in a safe house, a modest two story home the task force had secured for them on the island of Lido, a barrier island adjacent to Venice on its lagoon. They'd just updated Briggs, telling him where they were and what had happened back in Genoa.

Adrian and Nick were sharing one of the guest rooms, their window overlooking the nighttime waters of the lagoon that surrounded Lido. Her parents, hardly able to take their eyes off of each other, and Ivan, had each retired to their own guest rooms for the night after eating quick MRE's that were stored in the kitchen's pantry.

Before contacting Briggs, Adrian had also reached out to Polina and learned that Erasmo was fine, healing well from his gunshot wound. She and Sergey had taken him to a clinic on the mainland, over forty kilometers away on the outskirts of the city of Treviso, putting distance between themselves and Venice. They'd paid the doctor handsomely to not mention their presence there and to treat Erasmo after hours when the clinic was empty. The doctor insisted that Erasmo needed at least two nights of bed rest, which Erasmo was not happy about; he wanted to be here in Venice with them.

"Promise me you'll stop the bastards," he'd said, when Adrian had put him on speakerphone for her father.

"We will," her father had replied, his voice hard with determination.

"Speaking of my father," Adrian said now, heaving a sigh as she got to her feet. "I'm afraid you're going to have to deal with another episode of the stubborn Wests. I'm going to try to convince my parents to let us handle things going forward. They've been in enough danger. They need to stay here in the safe house before we can put them on a plane."

"Ha!" Nick said, looking genuinely amused. "Good luck with that. I'm coming with—I've got to see this."

Adrian shot him an annoyed but playful look, heading out of their room to make her way to her parents' guest room.

"Are you sure we're not interrupting them?" Nick asked, wriggling his eyebrows suggestively as they headed down the hall. "They haven't seen each other in over a decade. They have a lot to catch up on, if you get my—"

Adrian nudged him, letting out a groan. "Please don't put that image in my head," she muttered, wincing as she knocked on her parent's door.

To her relief, her mother opened it almost immediately. Cora pulled Adrian into her arms, her eyes shimmering with tears. "I still can't believe it, baby," she said when she pulled back.

"Me neither," Adrian said, her gaze straying to her father, who was standing behind her mother with a wide smile, and she momentarily forgot why she had come here.

"Mom, Dad," Adrian said finally, trying to put as much authority into her voice as she could, though being in the same room as both of her parents transported her back in time, and she suddenly felt like a child. "I'm going to insist that you stay here tomorrow. This is the last piece of the puzzle. Nick and I can take it from—"

"We've been over this, Adrian," Robert interrupted, his voice taking on that firm tone Adrian recalled from her very brief period of teenage rebellion. She half expected him to call her 'young lady'. "I'm not going anywhere until this is finished."

"Your father already tried to convince me to stay here—I'm tired of being a sitting duck. I'm not a fool, and I won't put myself in direct danger. Your father made me promise to run if it comes to it, and I know Ivan will protect me if necessary. All of you will. But I'm coming with you." Her mother's tone was just as firm. The emotion was gone from her eyes now, and she stood in a defensive, rigid stance. "I know this is your job, but—"

"Mom, you've already been abducted. And Dad, you know what they're capable of," Adrian protested.

"That is precisely why we're finishing this," Robert said, giving her a hard look. "I've already talked about this with your mother. This discussion is over."

Adrian glared at her parents, definitely feeling

like a child now. She wondered, defiantly, if she could force the issue by threatening to throw them both into protective custody, but her father's expression softened, and he stepped forward, gently squeezing her arms.

"You don't think I'm scared? The two great loves of my life are in this room. Everything I've done over the past decade has been to keep you both safe. You and I are so much alike, sweetheart. I'm not leaving anymore than you are."

"Can we just take this moment," Cora added, her tone gentle now as well, "to appreciate this moment? That we're all together again? This is a moment I never thought I'd—" Her voice broke.

Behind them, the door creaked open, and Adrian turned. Nick was trying to subtly slip out to give them privacy.

"You're not going anywhere, Nick," Cora said, dashing away her tears. "You're a part of this family—especially when you and Adrian give me grandchildren."

"Mom," Adrian gasped, mortified, but Nick just laughed.

"Agreed," Robert said, looping his arm around Cora's shoulders. "We know what we're up against, and the danger. But for the next—" he looked down at his phone—"hour, we're going to be a family and catch up. And then tomorrow, we're going to end this. Together."

After a tense beat, Adrian let her shoulders

relax. One hour. A reprieve. She could allow herself that.

They made their way down to the dining room, and after her mother prepared them all cups of tea, Adrian did something she thought she never would do again . . . have a conversation with both of her parents.

Robert didn't want to rehash his ten years of captivity with the Dieci, instead he wanted to hear as much details as possible about their lives during his absence.

And Adrian and Cora, with Nick pitching in at relevant points in the conversation, obliged. Adrian told him about her initial stint with the bureau, her decision to leave to go back into academia, and the Cleopatra case that had pulled her back into law enforcement.

Her mother told him about her and Adrian's relationship, the tension around Adrian's decision to work in law enforcement and her mother's eventual acceptance of it, how she had tried to move past her grief, and her persistent hope that Robert was still alive.

When they were done, it was late and fatigue had settled over them, but Adrian felt refreshed in a way she hadn't in a long time.

Before they retired to bed, she gave each parent a long hug. She was determined that no matter what tomorrow held, she would do whatever it took to ensure she'd never lose either of them again.

CHAPTER 37

Venice, Italy
9:02 AM

"They're heading toward the state archives," Bernardo said to Vittoria, from the other end of the line. "It's Adrian West, her parents, her partner, and Ivan Vasiliev."

Vittoria pressed her phone to her ear, excitement coursing through her at his words. She had just left her home and was approaching her private speedboat, flanked by several of her men.

Vittoria had her men monitor buildings in Venice that held historical records, just as she'd had them do in Istanbul, suspecting those were the places the Wests would go once they arrived. She'd known they would return to Venice ever since Sofia had confirmed that the letter led back here.

Their escape in Genoa had humiliated Vittoria, as she'd also learned from Sofia that the information they'd given her was false. It stung even more that the traitor Erasmo had helped them escape. She had been so desperate for answers that she'd allowed herself to be fooled.

Isabella had paid the ultimate price for Vittoria's foolhardiness; she hadn't survived her gunshot wound, and despite the efforts of the top doctors in Genoa, she'd succumbed to her injuries last night. Isabella had been a true believer of the cause. She had died for it, and Vittoria would make certain that her death was not in vain.

Unfortunately, Paolo Marini had found out about her failure in Genoa and left her a curt voice mail that morning, as she'd been avoiding his persistent texts and calls.

"I heard about the fiasco in Genoa. The other leaders and I are going to have an emergency meeting to discuss putting someone else on the trail of the key," he'd snapped.

Anger coursed through her at the memory; she wouldn't allow that. She would be the one to find the key, to move forward with the Dieci's plans. *Dalla distruzione alla rinascita.*

"Stay on them," Vittoria said now, stepping onto her boat and giving a nod to the driver. "*Do not* let them see you. We're going to let them lead us to the key . . . and then we're going to eliminate them."

9:15 AM

Like many buildings in Venice, the Archivio Di Stato Di Venezia, the State Archive of Venice, had been repurposed. It was once a Franciscan convent built during the thirteenth century. It became home to Venice's many records in the early nineteenth century. Located in the San Polo district, its piazza was the second largest in Venice, just after Saint Mark's Square.

The archives housed an astonishing amount of records, over seventy kilometers of shelves stuffed to the brim with documents from Venice's long history. Adrian and Nick had come here during their initial stay in Venice, but they hadn't even known where to begin to look. They didn't have enough information at the time.

They knew it was risky to come here, given that Vittoria and the Dieci were likely right on their tail, and the organization could very well have members who worked here. But this was the best place to get answers . . . somewhere in its mountains of records.

Adrian was glad that Ivan had suggested renting a private boat. There was less looking over her shoulder than if they had relied on the *vaparettos*, Venice's public water buses, or even *motoscafos*, water taxis. Ivan had rented a speedboat from a private owner early that morning, and turned out to be an exceptional boat driver, expertly managing the dips and swells of the lagoon, taking them from the Lido to the main island of Venice in less than an hour. He'd waved off their compliments, telling them that knowing how to operate a speedboat was often required in his security work.

Adrian and Robert entered the large neoclassical building of the archives that dominated the square. Ivan and Cora remained outside in front of the archives, keeping surveillance on who came in and out of the building. Her mother was visibly excited to be a part of their plan, and if Adrian wasn't so worried about her, she would have found it amusing. To her relief, her father had pulled Ivan aside, telling him to get Cora to safety at the first sign of any danger.

Nick was already inside; he'd entered before Adrian and Robert, surveilling the archives from the inside.

Adrian and her father approached one of the archivists for help, using the same cover story of being a professor and assistant that they'd used back in Istanbul. The archivist who helped them, Federico, was young and eager, a post-graduate student at The School of Archival Studies, Paleography and Diplomatics, which was housed in the building. He seemed genuine and Adrian didn't detect any deceptive behavior from him, but she was still on edge despite their precautions, terrified that Vittoria and her men would surround them at any moment.

After telling Federico what they were looking for, he led them to a large room next to one of the cloisters that the building surrounded, leaving them at a central table. Adrian was tense and alert as they waited, her eyes scanning the faces of each passerby, but no one paid them any mind. She remained tense even as Federico returned with a small stack of documents, handing them two sets of gloves as well.

"Here's a name I was able to find in the archives that's close to what you're looking for," Federico said. "Jacomo Chiaveno. His name was recorded in the guild of doctors and apothecaries that was established here in the thirteenth century."

Some of Adrian's tension faded, and she exchanged a hopeful look with her father. Jacomo Chiaveno. She had been right about his name. *The key*.

"Unfortunately, that's the only reference to him I could find," Federico continued, giving them an apologetic look, and Adrian's hope immediately faded. "He did have an apprentice listed alongside his name, and I recognized the name immediately—Rinaldo Calipiero. The Calipiero family was a wealthy shipbuilding family whose roots stretch back to the early days of Venice. Most family archives were dispersed after the fall of the Republic, but we have several documents from their family archives."

"Thank you," Robert said, and Federico left them alone.

Adrian looked down at the documents, discouraged. She didn't know how the apprentice's family records were going to help them, and defeat settled over her.

She thought about the letter Vittoria had them decode in Genoa. Her team could have successfully decoded it by now, which would lead the Dieci directly to the key.

"It's a start, sweetheart," Robert said, giving her a reassuring look.

Adrian wasn't feeling as optimistic, but for the next hour she and her father pored over the Calipiero family documents, their gloved hands sorting through each one, which were mostly property and financial records from their prosperous shipbuilding business during the height of the Republic. In spite of his apprenticeship, Rinaldo had not ended up going into medicine, and joined the family business instead. There were no other references to Chiaveno.

Picking up the final document, Rinaldo's will, Adrian scanned over it, defeat still weighing on her. Yet as she read over it . . .

She didn't know if it was just wishful thinking, but there was something off about the way the will was written. Adrian had studied medieval wills for lectures she'd done on language and death in the European Dark Ages, so she was familiar with their structure, which was why this one stood out as odd.

"Am I crazy?" she asked her father, handing him the document. "Or does the way this will is written seem off to you?"

"You're not crazy," Robert said slowly, scanning the will. "I've read plenty of wills from this time period. It's the preamble. It's much longer than usual and reads more like a confession."

Adrian nodded her agreement. Medieval wills were religious in nature, with a preamble committing the subject's soul to God, and they were often brief. The rest of the will designated where the writer wished to be buried, where donations were to be sent on his or her behalf—usually to a religious body such as a church or monastery—and property designations.

Rinaldo's will did have all of this . . . but the preamble took up most of the will. And there were parts of it that were vague and not as straightforward as other preambles she'd read, as if there were a hidden message buried within the words.

"What if—like the letter back in Genoa—Rinaldo didn't want to explicitly state something that the wrong eyes could see?" Adrian asked. "So he buried the message in his will, a document he knows will be preserved throughout time."

Adrian pointed to a section of the preamble that had immediately stood out for her, reading it out loud.

"Though the key may wish for its destruction, may God have mercy on my soul, the true key to preserving serenity is where the saint of death presides."

"Purposefully vague but rife with meaning," her father murmured. "And we have our key reference. As for 'where the saint of death presides' . . . I think that's significant as well."

"A location," Adrian suggested, excitement swirling in her veins.

She took out her phone, entering a search for 'saint of death' references and locations in Venice. Multiple hits came up, but one in particular stood out.

"Isola di San Michele," Adrian said, looking back up at her father. "It's an island in Venice's lagoon nicknamed the 'Cemetery Island'. It's named after Saint Michael. There's also a church named for him on the island. Saint Michael was guardian of the dead in the Roman Catholic religion."

"Saint Michael. Of course," her father said. "He's usually depicted holding scales on Judgement Day. In the Book of Revelations, he led the group of angels who defeated Satan, ejecting him from heaven. He appears to people when they die and offers them a chance of redemption before death."

Adrian and her father looked at each other, their excitement like an electric current between them.

They had found where the 'key', Jacomo Chiaveno, was likely buried.

CHAPTER 38

*A*drian stood at the head of the speedboat next to her parents and Nick as Ivan drove them away from Venice and north across the lagoon toward Isola di San Michele.

She'd read about the island on her phone during the brief journey. Since the early nineteenth century, the small island had served as the principal cemetery of Venice. The cemetery consisted of burial grounds for Catholics, with separate sections for Eastern Orthodox and Protestants. There was also the Chiesa di San Michele, a church considerably older than the cemetery itself, built during the fifteenth century. As a whole, the island was a place for the dead. Besides the cemetery and church, there was an ossuary and crematorium.

And possibly the key . . . the body of Jacomo Chiaveno.

"Robert. Adrian," Ivan said grimly. His eyes

were trained on the rear and side-view mirrors. "We are being followed."

Adrian stiffened, taking out the binoculars she'd brought and turning to scan the waters of the lagoon behind them.

Fear coiled around her spine; Ivan was right. In the near distance, two speedboats were heading right toward them.

Adrian set aside her fear as a hardened resolve settled over her. It was inevitable that the Dieci would find them here. Venice was their ancient headquarters, their territory.

"Everyone hold on. I will try to lose them," Ivan said, adjusting the throttle and picking up speed.

"Mom, Dad, get below deck," Adrian shouted, her heart hammering as she took out her gun and checked the chamber. She feared they would argue, especially her father, but Robert took her mother's hand and led her below deck to the small cabin without argument.

Nick came to her side, readying his weapon as well. Ivan picked up speed; he was heading back toward the main island of Venice. But he soon let out a curse, and Adrian followed his gaze. Yet another speedboat was approaching them from up ahead, also headed directly their way.

Ivan made an abrupt U turn, sending Adrian and Nick sprawling onto the deck. As she scrambled back to her feet, clutching on to the side of the boat, she realized with panic that the two boats were forcing them away from the relative safety of Venice's lagoon . . . out onto the open waters of the Adriatic.

Adrian braced herself on the side of the boat as Ivan picked up speed, Nick doing the same on the opposite side, raising their weapons. The three other speedboats were gaining on them, and she could make out a shooter on the closest one, stepping forward and raising his gun—

He fired. Adrian and Nick ducked before returning fire. Below deck, she heard her mother scream.

More bullets from the other boats were fired their way, and Ivan picked up even more speed. With the wind whipping her hair and sea spray splattering on her cheeks, Adrian continued to brace herself as she got to her knees, returning fire. But it was fruitless—they were outnumbered and the other boats were getting closer, almost on them.

As one of the boats got within firing range, Adrian fired off several shots, aiming for the driver, but he evaded, and the shooter next to him returned fire.

Adrian ducked as the second boat drew close. Nick fired, but he wasn't fast enough, and the shooter returned fire—aiming at Ivan—

The bullet struck him in the upper back, and he slumped over onto the deck. Panic crashed into her, and moving in a crouch, Adrian made her way to the steering wheel as Nick covered Ivan with his body, returning fire.

Adrian took control of the boat, grabbing the steering wheel, but the third boat had pulled up alongside them. She looked around for an escape route, but they were surrounded. She was forced to bring the boat to a stop.

Vittoria emerged from behind the driver of the first boat, giving her a chilly smile.

CHAPTER 39

12:46 PM

Since returning to the bureau, Adrian had lost count of how many times someone had aimed a gun at her, or how many times she'd been shot at.

This was the first time, however, that she couldn't care less about her own life.

Her focus was centered entirely on her parents, who were being marched separately onto Isola di San Michele from Vittoria's boat. Vittoria had a man on each of them, a pistol pressed into their backs.

Vittoria herself walked next to Adrian, her gun jabbed painfully into Adrian's side as she was forced to trail her parents. Nick was right behind them, with another one of Vittoria's men shadowing him. Vittoria and her men had concealed their weapons with their jackets.

From her vantage point, she could see a handful of tourists wandering the island's cemetery; she didn't dare attempt to get their attention.

"If you make one wrong move, I promise you will watch your mother die," Vittoria had hissed, and Adrian believed her.

Ivan was on one of Vittoria's boats below deck, alive, but in a great deal of pain, barely clinging to consciousness. Adrian had feared Vittoria would execute him outright; she had instead kept him alive, having one of her men staunch his bleeding wound before standing guard over him. Adrian realized with dread that Vittoria was using his life as leverage, in addition to her parents' and Nick's.

Frustration arose in Adrian's gut; she should have forced her parents to stay behind. Now both of their lives were in danger, and Adrian didn't know how she was going to get them out of this.

After surrounding their boat, Vittoria had made them tell her everything they'd learned. With guns aimed at her parents and Nick, Adrian had told her everything, not holding anything back. Vittoria seemed satisfied with her answers, and they were now headed to the ossuary on the island to seek out Chiaveno's remains.

Given how old his remains were, he wasn't buried in the cemetery, of which the earliest burials were from the nineteenth century. His remains had likely been transferred to the ossuary on the island, along with the older remains, which was where they were going to search.

For a cemetery island, Isola di San Michele was lush with carefully tended trees and greenery, with the trees surrounding the cemetery like sentries guarding the dead.

They made their way down a path that wound around the cemetery toward the ossuary. She felt as if they were being marched to their doom. Adrian forced herself to keep her breathing steady, though panic scorched her veins. She needed to focus, and that required calm. Right now, the best way to keep the people she loved alive was to remain useful to Vittoria.

Once they arrived at the ossuary, Vittoria ordered her men to spread out and search, keeping their captives close at hand.

Vittoria turned to Adrian, narrowing her eyes. "If any of them attempt any move whatsoever, shoot them."

Chiaveno isn't here.

The realization slowly dawned on Adrian as they spent the next two hours searching the ossuary, to no avail.

Vittoria even had one of her men inquire about burials at the church on the island, the Chiesa di San Michele, which was considerably older than both the cemetery and the ossuary. But there were no remains buried there.

Vittoria's fury was palpable. She marched

Adrian to the edge of the ossuary, pressing her weapon so firmly into Adrian's side that she winced in pain. Nick lurched forward with a snarl, her mother whimpered with fear and her father went rigid, but the men on them held them all back.

"Was this another trick, like back in Genoa? Do you think I'm a fool?" Vittoria snapped.

"I told you everything," Adrian said through clenched teeth, struggling to keep her voice steady.

Vittoria studied her for a long time, as if determining the veracity of her words, before turning to her men. "Take them back to the boat," she barked. She gave Adrian a look that chilled her to the bone. "It will be easier to dump their bodies in the sea."

Terror ripped through Adrian as the men marched them off the island and back onto Vittoria's boat.

Think. What had they gotten wrong? She thought again of the line in the will they had focused on. *Though the key may wish for its destruction, may God have mercy on my soul, the true key to preserving serenity is where the saint of death presides.*

What was she missing?

She repeated the line to herself as they were dragged down to the lower deck of Vittoria's boat. Once they were all gathered in the cramped space, Vittoria lifted her gun, released the safety, and aimed it at her mother's head.

Robert let out a cry of fury and stumbled

forward, but his guard punched him in the gut, making him keel over.

"This is the wrong place, and I think you know that," Vittoria hissed. "This will prove to you that I make good on my threats."

Her next move seemed to happen in slow motion.

Vittoria turned her gun on Robert, aiming for his chest, and pulled the trigger.

CHAPTER 40

Her mother screamed, and shock descended over Adrian as her father slumped to the floor of the deck.

Vittoria turned, calmly aiming her weapon at Cora.

Adrian felt the world around her shift, her shock giving way to panic. Her father was unconscious, his breathing faint as blood seeped through the fabric of his shirt to the deck. *So much blood,* she thought dimly, feeling as if she were watching from a distance as two of Vittoria's men lifted her father's still body, disappearing with him to a back room.

"Now. Where should we really be looking, or do I shoot your mother and your lover as well?"

During her time at the FBI Academy, Adrian had learned a concentration exercise. The other agents in training would surround the trainee, doing anything they could to distract them while the trainee focused on completing an assigned task. It was designed to teach the trainees to maintain their calm and focus during intense and potentially deadly situations. At the time, Adrian had thought the exercise was a little useless, but she was now glad she had that training in her back pocket.

She used it now, honing all her focus on the problem and solution. She eliminated everything else in her physical perimeter—Vittoria's gun aimed at her mother, her mother's sobs, her father's blood staining the deck. Nick struggling against the man who held him, his eyes wild.

Problem. Solution. Problem—they had gone to the wrong place. They had focused too much on Saint Michael. But there were plenty of other places that Rinaldo Calipiero's will could refer to.

Though the key may wish for its destruction, may God have mercy on my soul, the true key to preserving serenity is where the saint of death presides.

The saint of death presides. She mentally reviewed the other possibilities she and the others had considered before settling on Saint Michael.

"I'm getting impatient, Adrian," Vittoria snapped, stepping closer to her mother.

Adrian kept her panic at bay, maintaining her focus, until one place sprang forward in her mind.

"Lazaretto Vecchio," Adrian said.

Lazaretto Vecchio, which translated to Old Lazaret—old quarantine station—was an island that served as a leper colony from the fifteenth to seventeenth centuries. Most crucially, it hospitalized the ill during waves of plague epidemics that hit Venice, and to this day mass and individual graves of plague victims were being unearthed there.

"Lazaretto was derived from the Biblical name of Lazarus," Adrian continued. "He became free of death, raised from the dead. Presiding—it can be seen as ruling over or winning over death. It's something the Venetians were trying to do by using the plague to vanquish their enemies."

Vittoria was listening intently, though she still kept her weapon aimed at Cora. Once again, Adrian felt the panic bleed in. She took a breath and willingly held it at bay, as if putting up an emotional dam, as she continued, "Let's assume Chiaveno dies when the plague comes to Venice in 1348. We know from the records that his apprentice, Rinaldo Calipiero, is only twenty when he dies. Calipiero doesn't die until 1408. On Lazaretto Vecchio, there was a hospital that took in plague victims and sufferers of leprosy at this time. Calipiero had the means to have Chiaveno's body transferred from its original burial place and buried there."

"Lazaretto Vecchio is one of the places the Dieci has searched over the years," Vittoria said, though she looked conflicted. "Nothing has ever been found."

"We need to look again," Adrian said firmly. "Bodies of plague victims have been found there over the years—it makes the most sense."

Again, Vittoria studied Adrian for a disconcertingly long time. Adrian held her gaze, though she was terrified that Vittoria would still shoot her mother just to prove a point.

Finally, Vittoria turned to one of her men, barking an order in rapid Italian.

When she turned back to Adrian, her voice was cold. "This is your last chance. You should pray that the key is there."

CHAPTER 41

Venetian Lagoon
4:19 PM

The journey from Isola di San Michele to Lazaretto Vecchio was only half an hour, but it felt like days. Months. Years.

A multitude of emotions flowed through Adrian—fear for her parents, Nick, and Ivan, worry that she was wrong, frustration for not going to Lazaretto Vecchio first.

Yet her worry was ultimately pointless. If she was right and they found the body, Vittoria would kill them. If she was wrong, she would kill them. From what she could recall about Lazaretto Vecchio, it was generally closed to tourists, only opening occasionally for guided tours. It was the perfect place to kill them before disposing of their bodies in the lagoon.

She tried not to think of her father bleeding to

death, or of Vittoria executing her mother and Nick. She suspected—hoped—that Vittoria was keeping her father alive, like Ivan, as leverage—but that would only last for so long.

Adrian stood at the head of the boat next to Vittoria as it headed south to Lazaretto Vecchio. Vittoria was glued to her side, her pistol rammed against Adrian's ribcage. Nick and her mother were behind her, two of Vittoria's men on them as well.

She subtly took in the number of men Vittoria had with her. Between this boat and the other two that trailed them, Adrian counted seven men. She could only pray that Vittoria didn't have even more men patrolling the surrounding lagoon.

Adrenaline rushed through Adrian's veins as they neared the island of Lazaretto Vecchio. The island was their only chance of escape.

Their boat pulled up to a landing dock, and Vittoria nudged Adrian forward. "Go," she snapped.

Adrian stepped onto the dock. Behind her, the two men on Cora and Nick forced them off the boat as well.

She looked around, taking in the island. It was small, only slightly over six acres. Unlike Isola di San Michele, with its lush greenery and well-tended grounds, Lazaretto Vecchio looked desolate, with crumbling buildings taking up half the island, while the other half was under construction for an intended museum. Nature was reclaiming many of the buildings—overgrown grasses and the winding branches of unkempt trees were curling around them.

"Where are we looking?" Vittoria demanded with narrowed eyes, the question sounding more like a threat.

"You mentioned the Dieci has checked here before. Where have they looked?" Adrian asked.

"Whenever the bones of plague victims have been recovered, we search for any hint of virulent strains extracted from their bones. And we monitor what is found during excavations all over the island," Vittoria replied, gesturing around at the buildings that dotted Lazaretto Vecchio.

It sounded to Adrian like the Dieci hadn't thoroughly searched the island at all, but she was certainly not going to point that out. Instead, she said, "I don't think Rinaldo Calipiero would have had Chiaveno's body buried in a mass grave with other plague victims. I also doubt it would be found in a regular individual grave. According to the wording in his will, he wanted the body preserved, despite Chiaveno's wishes."

Adrian turned to again face the decrepit buildings of the island, recalling what she knew about it. For centuries it had served as a place for the sick—a leper colony as well as a hospital for plague victims. Her gaze landed on one building in the near distance as she recalled one particular fact.

"There was a special hospital here reserved just for nobles," Adrian said slowly. "I think we should start there."

After a tense beat, Vittoria roughly shoved her forward and turned to face her men. "Bernardo, Isaac, Giancarlo, Luca, and Jon are coming with us. Enzo and David, you two stay with the boats."

Adrian noticed that two of the men, Isaac and Giancarlo, each had handheld GPR scanners, ground penetrating devices that could detect hidden areas beneath building structures.

They made their way away from the dock, cutting a path through the overgrown grasses. Some buildings they passed were intact; she knew that these were the regular hospital and staff building.

They continued until they reached the hospital for nobles, the top half of which was relatively intact while the bottom was partially caved in and overrun with wild plants and trees that threatened to consume it.

Cautiously, they entered, taking the uneven stairs to the top half of the hospital. The interior held no trace of the hospital it had once been, consisting of only cracked stone floors and walls.

Vittoria nudged Adrian inside, keeping her gun pressed against her back. Her men did the same with her mother and Nick.

"Search everywhere," Vittoria ordered her men.

Isaac and Giancarlo spread out, scanning the walls and floors with their devices.

Adrian watched them, tense, wondering if now was the time to make her move. Isaac and Giancarlo were distracted with the scanners. The other two, Luca and Jon, were on her mother and

Nick, and Vittoria had ordered the last one, Bernardo, to stand guard outside. With her and Nick, that was two to five. Not great odds, but doable if they could get their hands on their weapons.

She decided against acting for now—she was too far away from Nick to communicate her intentions. He was on the other side of the room with her mother. And while Vittoria was focused intently on her men scanning the room, she wasn't distracted enough for Adrian to make a move.

But Adrian knew she needed to act fast. She could tell Vittoria's patience was hanging by the thinnest of threads . . . if nothing was found here, Vittoria could kill her mother or Nick purely out of rage.

Isaac and Giancarlo scanned every square inch of the room, and Adrian's unease increased. Finally, Isaac turned to face Vittoria. "It doesn't look like there's anything here."

Vittoria's jaw clenched. She glanced down at the crumbling stone floor. "Then we need to check below."

Isaac hesitated. "It's not a very secure area. Maybe we can—"

"I didn't ask you if it was a secure area. I told you we need to check below," Vittoria snapped.

Isaac lowered his gaze, giving her a gruff nod. He and Giancarlo left the room, heading back down the uneven stairs.

"Move," Vittoria barked, nudging Adrian

forward with her gun. Adrian headed out, her heart pounding with fear.

They made their way down the stairs and entered the decrepit first floor. Isaac was right. With uneven stone floors covered with rubble and partially caved in walls, this area looked as if it were on the verge of collapse.

But Vittoria didn't seem to care, her dark eyes focused intently on the two men as they began to carefully move around the room, scanning each section.

Adrian swallowed, meeting Nick's eyes across the room. She wondered if he was thinking the same thing. Now, when they were in this precarious room, was the time to act.

But just as she was about to make a move—

A piercing blare filled the room, and Adrian stiffened. Giancarlo had detected something. He was standing in the far corner of the room, next to a pile of rubble. Excitement gleamed in Vittoria's eyes as Giancarlo knelt, running his scanner over the ground, and the alarm increased in volume.

Something was down there.

Isaac and Giancarlo cleared away the rubble using their hands and feet, gradually revealing a stone floor below. It was cracked and hollowed out, looking as if it were on the verge of caving in.

Vittoria nodded at Isaac, and he stood back, firing several bullets into the floor. It caved in with a splintering groan, revealing a narrow passageway about four feet below them.

Isaac knelt, shining a flashlight into it. From her vantage point, Adrian could see that the passageway was long, winding further ahead beneath the building.

It was the perfect place to hide a preserved body. A tomb.

Vittoria smiled, her eyes shining with a dark hunger. "Adrian and I will go down first—the two of you will come with us." She turned to Jon and Luca, the men guarding Nick and her mother. "Stay up here. If they blink wrong, shoot them."

Vittoria turned her focus to Adrian. "After you," she said coldly.

In the next few seconds, Adrian made a decision.

If Chiaveno's burial place was down there, Vittoria would kill them all, having no use for them anymore. If Chiaveno wasn't down there, Vittoria would still kill them all out of sheer frustration. Her instincts told her that if she went into that tunnel now . . . she wouldn't come back out.

And so she acted, knowing that it was now or never.

CHAPTER 42

In a rapid fire move, Adrian lowered herself down to a crouch and kicked out at Vittoria's legs, sending her hurtling into the passageway below, her gun slipping out of one of her hands as she threw both of them out to break her fall.

"Mom, get down!" Adrian shouted, catching Vittoria's gun. She whirled to aim the gun at Jon and Luca, the guards who'd released Cora and Nick and were racing toward her, their own weapons raised—

Her mother obliged, throwing herself to the ground as Adrian shot the two guards, sending them crumpling to the ground.

Nick moved fast, grabbing the weapon of one of the downed guards as Bernardo, who had been standing outside, raced in, raising his weapon. Nick fired two shots at Bernardo as Adrian whirled toward Giancarlo and Isaac, who charged toward her—

Isaac fired at her, but Adrian dodged, and Nick fired two bullets at his chest. Isaac crumpled as Giancarlo aimed to shoot Adrian, but she was faster, raising her weapon and firing off a shot.

As Giancarlo slumped to the ground, Adrian straightened, her breath heaving, peering down into the passageway. There was no sign of Vittoria, and panic flared in her belly. She turned to Nick.

"Get my mother out of here and call for backup—my dad and Ivan need medical attention immediately," Adrian said. She didn't wait for Nick to protest, which she knew he would, and lowered herself into the passageway.

She darted down the passageway, clutching Vittoria's gun and searching the darkness for any sign of her. The further she went into the passageway, the darker it became, and she desperately wished she had a flashlight. The passageway seemed endless, even though the hospital above wasn't very large, making her suspect it had been here long before the hospital had been built.

Adrian kept moving at a jog, the gun out and at the ready, scanning every inch of the darkness for Vittoria, but she saw no sign of her.

Eventually, Adrian came to a dead end. The passageway stretched both left and right, each way leading into more inky darkness. Adrian looked back and forth, uncertain of which way to go, listening for any sign of Vittoria . . .

As she turned to scan the left side of the passageway, one of the shadows behind her *moved*.

It was Vittoria, who lunged at her from the darkness.

∼

Five Minutes Ago

VITTORIA RACED down the dark passageway, her breathing thunderous in her own ears. The gunshots above her were rapid; she feared West and her partner had taken all of her men down. She kept running, determined to find a way out.

Vittoria . . .

The voice was a whisper. Her husband Ben's voice. She almost stopped, but willed herself to keep moving.

Mama . . .

Her son's voice. Massimo. Vittoria halted, tears pricking her eyes, scanning the darkness. She had to remind herself that her son couldn't be here . . . he was gone. Forcing back a sob, Vittoria again took off at a run.

She needed to focus. She'd left two of her men back at the boat—they could kill Adrian and the others. Vittoria could call for backup from the Dieci, get the key, take it back to her lab. Complete the plan.

She was close. So close. Jacomo Chiaveno's tomb was nearby . . . she could feel it.

Mama.

Vittoria ignored the whisper. Massimo was gone. Her husband was gone. Her two loves, taken by the corruption of this world.

Tori. This isn't who you are. Don't do this.

Ben again. But it wasn't Ben. He was dead. They were the reason she was doing this . . . had to do this.

Don't do this.

I have to do this, Vittoria wanted to shout. She had to bite her lip to keep from letting out a cry that would give away her location.

Vittoria halted when she came to a dead end, looking around in frustration. She could hear footsteps behind her, closing in. She had no doubt that it was Adrian, and she was getting closer.

Vittoria tucked herself away in the shadows of the passageway, feeling around on the ground for any sort of weapon she could use against the bitch. She found some stones on the ground. Not ideal, but they would have to do.

Gripping a stone in her hand, she pushed herself back against the wall.

And she waited.

Seconds later, Adrian approached the same dead end, halting in her tracks and looking around.

Vittoria didn't waste a second. She lunged forward, raising the stone above her head to slam it down onto Adrian's head, but the other woman dodged, slipping on another loose stone. Vittoria took advantage of this, reaching for her gun.

They struggled with it; Vittoria head butted her, and when Adrian loosened her grip on the weapon, Vittoria snatched it away. She aimed and fired, but again Adrian dodged, and the bullet struck her in the shoulder.

Adrian let out a cry of pain, stumbling back. Vittoria fired again, missing the other woman as she expertly rolled out of the way. This time, Vittoria's bullet struck the wall behind her.

The wall let out a creaking groan. Vittoria stumbled back, both terrified and astonished, as it crumbled in on itself, revealing . . .

A small, cavernous room. This wall wasn't a dead end. It was a cover. A seal. Because deep inside the room . . . there was a stone sarcophagus.

Vittoria neatly stumbled to her knees. It was here. Chiaveno's body. The key.

But first, she needed to take care of a nuisance. She whirled, searching the passageway, but Adrian had disappeared.

Her pulse racing, Vittoria searched the darkness, the shadows. But there was no one. Until—

Adrian emerged from behind Vittoria, hefting a large, shattered piece of the crumpled stone wall. Vittoria raised her weapon, but she wasn't fast enough.

Adrian slammed the stone down onto Vittoria's head, and pain exploded in her temple as her world dissolved to black.

Adrian stumbled back from Vittoria's still form, her breathing labored. She leaned back against the wall, closing her eyes, clutching her bleeding shoulder, wincing against the pain.

Gritting her teeth, she ripped off the bottom half of her shirt, hissing as she pressed the fabric to her bleeding wound. She then carefully stepped into the cavernous room, making her way toward the stone sarcophagus.

Grunting with effort and ignoring the pain in her shoulder, she shoved the top of the sarcophagus partially aside, awe descending over at the sight of what was inside.

CHAPTER 43

One Day Later
Venice, Italy
3:28 PM

Adrian and Nick stood over the sarcophagus of Jacomo Chiaveno, with Polina and Erasmo hovering behind them, all wearing protective gear. A local team of anthropologists and paleopathologists had taken off the top of the sarcophagus, revealing Chiaveno's remains inside.

His body had been wrapped in waxed cloth for preservation. He had a tall frame for the time at slightly over six feet, and his build was slender. A full genetic analysis was needed to confirm that it was Chiaveno, but they had done a preliminary estimate that he was a male in his late forties when he died, likely of the plague from the state of his remains, which tracked with what they knew of Chiaveno, who would have been forty-eight at the time the Black Death swept over Venice.

"I can't believe this corpse is over six hundred years old," Nick muttered, shaking his head.

"Whoever preserved him did a good job for the fourteenth century," Polina said. "I think an ethanol solution was used called aqua vita, before his body was wrapped with waxed cloth."

Adrian glanced back at Erasmo and Polina with a smile, glad that they were able to see the 'key' that they had helped search for.

The previous day, shortly after Adrian peered down into Chiavano's sarcophagus, she'd heard Nick's frantic voice shouting her name as he raced down the passageway with several Venetian police officers. He'd used the phone of one of Vittoria's fallen men to call both the local authorities and Briggs, and in only a matter of minutes, the Venetian police were swarming Lazaretto Vecchio. They had taken the two men guarding Vittoria's boat into custody, and Ivan and Robert were immediately transferred to a local hospital.

The police had taken away the bodies of Vittoria's men, and Vittoria, who had survived the blow Adrian dealt her, but remained unconscious, was taken to the hospital under police guard. Adrian herself was treated for her shoulder injury on site, but refused a hospital bed for further rest and recovery, to Nick's chagrin.

Instead, she'd gone to the hospital to wait with her mother, holding her hand, while doctors performed surgery on her father. To her immense relief, he had survived his gunshot wound, with Vittoria's bullet just missing his heart and other vital organs, but he'd needed a transfusion and would be in the hospital for a few more days for rest and observation.

She and Nick had then paid a visit to Ivan, who thankfully also survived his gunshot wound. Like her father, he was unconscious and resting when they visited, so Adrian had just taken his hand and squeezed it, murmuring a thanks to him for keeping her mother—and the rest of them—safe.

Adrian and the others had given their statements to the local police and had debriefed Briggs, but there would be more follow up when they returned to DC—especially for her father once he recovered.

The authorities had sealed off the tomb and a local team of paleopathologists and anthropologists were handling the processing of Chiaveno's body. They were the ones who had invited Adrian to have one last look into the tomb before his body was taken away; Adrian had insisted the others who had assisted in the search be allowed to view it as well.

It hadn't taken long for a fully recovered

Erasmo and Polina to join them, and after Erasmo had visited her father and Ivan in the hospital, they had all made their way back to Lazaretto Vecchio.

"So. This is the 'key' that's been causing all this trouble," Erasmo said, taking in Chiaveno's body with a wry grin.

"The one and only," Nick said.

As Adrian's eyes roamed over Jacomo Chiaveno's body, she wondered what the last moments of life had been like. Had he felt culpable for the death that was sweeping over the streets of Venice at the time? Polina and the local paleopathologists believed he'd died somewhere else, possibly to prevent his body from being used for precisely what the Dieci intended to do.

But his apprentice had likely found him not long after he died and had his body preserved against Chiaveno's wishes, before later moving him to this hidden tomb for the Dieci to use if necessary in the future . . . but its precise location was lost with time.

"We need to process the remains," the lead paleopathologist, Bianca, said from behind them, interrupting Adrian's train of thought. "I'm afraid it's time for you all to leave."

The others, except for Nick, turned to leave. Adrian's gaze remained on Jacomo Chiaveno . . . the key the Dieci had been seeking for centuries. It seemed he had tried to do the right thing at the end. If Vittoria and the Dieci had succeeded . . .

She shuddered at the thought. They hadn't succeeded, and that was all that mattered.

Adrian took one last lingering look at Chiaveno's remains before taking Nick's extended hand and leaving the tomb, and the key, behind.

CHAPTER 44

One Month Later
Alexandria, Virginia
6:17 PM

"So. What should we toast to?" Cora asked, looking around the dining room table at Adrian, Nick and Robert.

Adrian grinned at her mother, raising her wineglass. "To family," she said, meeting her father's gaze.

"I'll drink to that," her father returned, and they clinked their glasses together.

It had been a tumultuous few weeks since they'd left Venice. Her father had been in and out of debriefings and intense questioning with the task force and other international law enforcement agencies, detailing everything he knew about the Dieci and what he'd done for them during his captivity. Feeling protective of her father, Adrian had initially urged Briggs and the other law enforcement agents to give him time to reintegrate back into society and recover from his gunshot wound.

Her father had insisted he wanted to help—and the sooner, the better. In a way, it was like an exorcism of all he'd gone through. The authorities here in DC had even reopened their investigation into his friend Niles Harrington's death.

Robert was slowly easing back into the life he'd left behind. He'd told them he eventually wanted to return to work in academia, but Adrian and Cora insisted he take much needed time off before doing so. Adrian knew that would be an uphill battle . . . she'd inherited her workaholic tendencies from her father. For now, her mother told her they spent their days taking long walks, talking, reconnecting. He had even agreed to see a therapist to begin processing the psychological toll his captivity had taken on him.

Looking at her father now, an array of emotions coursed through her. For so long, a reunion like this had seemed impossible. But her father was alive, here in the flesh, and they were a complete family again. Nick reached out to squeeze her hand, reading her thoughts like always.

Adrian's thoughts turned to the events back in Europe. Right now, Athena Karras was working with the authorities in Italy, sharing the intel she had on the Greek branch, Archaia Sofia. Vittoria was in custody on a barrage of charges. They'd learned more about her since her capture, how she'd lost her son and husband in a suicide bombing, an event that set Vittoria on her destructive path. The authorities had located and shut down her lab in Geneva, questioning the workers Vittoria had employed there and making arrests where necessary.

Erasmo was working alongside the authorities, and Ivan was providing input as well. With Erasmo, Ivan and her father's input, the Italian authorities had made at least a dozen arrests of Dieci members, with more forthcoming. With Vittoria's arrest and the arrests of its other leaders, the Dieci was in shambles, just as they'd aimed for.

Ivan had fully recovered from his gunshot wound and had reunited with his son; he'd sent a photo of them together to Cora and the others, which had made tears spring to her mother's eyes.

Polina had also helped provide evidence to the authorities and was now back at the institute in Bucharest. Mikhail and Florin had been placed under arrest, with Mikhail losing his position at the institute, and Polina was promoted to take over his position.

As for Jacomo's body, a genetic analysis had confirmed his identity by linking to a current, living relative. A more virulent strain of Yersinia pestis, the strain Vittoria and the Dieci had been searching for, had caused his death. The authorities had reburied his remains, its location kept under wraps for security reasons.

They were opening up another bottle of wine when Adrian's phone rang. She looked down at it, frowning. It was Briggs. She glanced over at Nick, who gave her a look of concern.

Cora sighed. "I would tell you no work calls at the table, but now that I know what your job is like . . ."

Adrian stood, offering her parents an apologetic smile. "We'll try to make this quick."

She and Nick left her parents in the dining room, moving to the privacy of the study as Adrian answered, placing the call on speaker.

"I'm sorry to bother you both," Briggs said, his voice tense. "But I'm in Mexico City. I flew down last night. We have a . . . situation. I need both of you to fly down here ASAP."

∽

The adventure continues in Book Five, THE CARIBBEAN CODE.

THE CARIBBEAN CODE

An ancient code. A looming danger. A powerful secret that can change the world--or end it...

The adventure continues in Book 5 of the Adrian West Adventures series.

AUTHOR'S NOTE

I've had the pleasure of visiting Venice twice, but it has fascinated me long before my visits. I remember reading in travel books and magazines about this floating, magical city nestled among the lagoons. Before my first visit, I even read about the city's origins, from refugees fleeing barbarian invaders to the lagoons just after the fall of Rome, to its height as a maritime empire.

Due to my long fascination with the city, I knew I wanted to set one of Adrian's adventures there. If Adrian calls it the Timeless City, I call it the Magical City; there is something otherworldly about a city nestled among islands in a lagoon, somehow both a part of the land and the sea, surviving for centuries against great odds.

As a powerful maritime city during the medieval era, the infamous Black Plague hit Venice hard. Our word 'quarantine' comes from the Venetians' isolation of travelers to prevent the spread of

AUTHOR'S NOTE

illness during this dark time. The deadly epidemic had raged throughout Europe multiple times over the centuries, but most notably in 1348.

The coded letters Adrian, her father and Nick decode in Dubrovnik and later Genoa are both fictional, but they are based on actual coded letters sent in the ancient and medieval world.

In Dubrovnik, the locations Adrian and Nick go to, from Saint Blaise's Church to the Revelin Fortress are actual places just as I described. The locations they visit in Istanbul also exist, from Zeyrek Mosque to Tekfur Palace, though I did add a fictional museum for Zeyrek Mosque and a fictional records room for Tekfur Palace.

Maria of Antioch was a real historical person, as was Emperor Andronikos. I did, however, invent the mention of a mysterious doctor.

The institute where Polina works in Bucharest is fictional, though I did base it on actual archaeological institutes that are responsible for locating and analyzing archaeological finds.

Vittoria's villa in Genoa is fictional, but the affluent Albaro district is a real location, as is the Palazzo Ducale, which really does have underground tunnels not open to the public.

The Genoan Vincitori family and the Venetian Calipiero families are both my invention, though I did based them on powerful maritime families from the height of these two cities' affluence during the medieval era.

The locations Adrian and the others go to in

Venice all exist as well—the state archives, Lido Island, Isola di San Michele and Lazaretto Vecchio. For Lazaretto Vecchio, I did take some license around the hospital for nobles, which really does exist on the island, by adding the underground passageway and the decrepit lower level.

The ancient secret society of the Dieci is, of course, fictional, but Venice during its height was filled to the brim with secrets and spies. In fact, the motto for Venice's official Council of Ten was *jura, perjura, secretum prodere noli*. Swear, foreswear and reveal not the secret. I don't think it's too far-fetched for a secret society—or societies—to have once existed there.

As for biological warfare, there is historical record of it being used around the time of the plague. Just before the Black Death spread across Europe, there was in fact a siege in Kaffa, modern day Feodosia, during which the Mongol army infected the city's inhabitants with the bodies of their dead, contributing to the spread of the plague in Europe.

As I mention in the novel, there is also record of a Venetian doctor who wanted to use the 'quintessence' of plague against Venice's enemies during the Venetian Ottoman war.

There were different strains of the bacterium that caused the Black Death, including more virulent ones as I mention in the novel, and pairing such a pathogen with a virus would indeed be apocalyptic. And mass graves of plague victims are

AUTHOR'S NOTE

still being found to this day, including on Lazaretto Vecchio.

I used many resources in my research for this novel, but a couple of my most helpful resources include *Venice* by Peter Ackroyd and *City of Fortune* by Roger Crowley, both fascinating reads in their own right.

A sincere thanks to you, dear reader, for joining Adrian's latest adventure. We're leaving Europe for her next adventure, and I hope you'll come along for the ride.

Until next time,
—L.D.G.
2023

ABOUT THE AUTHOR

L.D. Goffigan writes fast-paced thrillers and action-adventure with historical intrigue. She studied film and dramatic writing at New York University and currently divides her time between France and California.

When not writing, you can find her traveling to places she's never been, reading the latest book which strikes her fancy, or watching a documentary about ancient mysteries.

To be notified about new releases, visit L.D. Goffigan's website to join her newsletter. Subscribers are also alerted to giveaways and exclusive bonus content.

Stay in touch!
ld@ldgoffiganbooks.com
ldgoffiganbooks.com

www.ingramcontent.com/pod-product-compliance
Lightning Source LLC
LaVergne TN
LVHW091720070526
838199LV00050B/2474

9 7 9 8 9 9 0 2 3 4 4 3 7